Waterbury Tales

Three-Word Stories:
One Tale

Noland T. Williams

Blue M Publishing, LLC - CHICAGO

Library of Congress Cataloging-in-publication data
Names: Noland T. Williams
Title: *Waterbury Tales. – Three Word Stories – One Tale.*
Description: First edition | Blue M Publishing, Chicago, IL [2018] | Single Book | Contents: Three-Word Stories | Summary: A coach full of travelers becomes stranded in the middle of nowhere when their bus breaks down. Then, a mysterious passerby steps out of the woodlands to help them. But before he does, he asks each passenger to tell a story. | Audience Note: Recommended for readers thirteen and older | Language Note: Infrequent offensive language.
Identifiers: ISBN 978-1-945385-17-9 (Paperback)
Subjects: LCSH: sh85048050 Fiction; sh85121965 | BISAC FIC014050 | GSAFD:
Classification: LCC PS370-380 | DDC 813/--dc23

Waterbury Tales –Three Word Stories – One Tale.
Noland T. Williams
ISBN 978-1-945385-17-9 (Paperback)

Printed in the United States of America
www.blueMpublishing.com
Book Cover Design by Allendorf-Vignere

Blue M Publishing
19 South Stough Street, Suite 100
Hinsdale, IL 60521

Rating: PG13 Parental Guidance for readers under thirteen years of age for use of harsh language and images of violence or threats of violence. No drug or alcohol use is described. There are no scenes with sexual references or implied sexual activity.

Waterbury Tales
Three-Word Stories – One Tale

Book Summary

It all began with a simple coach trip in England, spanning the countryside through the emerald green rolling hills to the intended destination of Waterbury. However, as all things happen, the journey was interrupted by unforeseen events.

Much like those who embarked on Chaucer's trek through *Canterbury Tales*, the passengers pass the time by engaging in a friendly game of storytelling. Each is asked to weave a story using three words they pull randomly from a dirty, brown sock cap. The story that evolves is captivating. Yet, they soon realize that the end of their story does not conclude their odyssey. There is much more of their own story left to be told.

*****

Waterbury Tales

Contents

Preface

Two confluent themes in my life as an author come forward in this unusual story. The first is rather simplistic. When my daughter was about five, I would put her to bed, and she would insist that I tell her a story. We would often read a story from a children's book, but sometimes she would want me to make-up one for her. Each time, I would ask her to help me by giving me three words that form the basis for the story. During the next couple of years, the three words got harder to embed into a single tale, and I would ask for her help.

In addition, my father served as a lieutenant in the U.S. Navy during World War II. He had many tales to tell about his missions in the South Pacific and what life was like in those days. Even into his nineties, these tales were some of his only surviving memories as Alzheimer's slowly stole from him his treasured past. Although in his later years, he struggled to recall my name, he always retained the vivid imagery of those years he spent on the high seas off the coast of Iwo Jima, Midway, and mainland Japan.

This story combines the two. While the tale is interesting and very loosely reflects the events of the 1940s (due to the nature of the characters and the word usage), the mode of delivery is unique. One must follow the characters who have been assembled on the journey to understand from where the words were derived and the story ultimately spun.

Not an easy tale to tell with such constraints, I attempted to pull together a tale to honor those in the greatest of generations – those who suffered through the Great Depression and World War II – as well as those who offer hope for a better future – my daughter and her generation. I leave the success of this attempt to you, the reader, but my motives were … honorable.

Since beginning to write this book, my beloved father passed away at the age of ninety-five. He was never able to read it, but I often told him that I loved him and that his generation was, indeed, the greatest that had ever graced our country. Of course, homage is required to certain other generations – those that fought in the Revolutionary War and Civil War, but in more recent times, those who fought in WWI and WWII are some of the greatest Americans of our time.

So, this one's for you, Dad.

Introduction

The idea for writing this book came from the writer's interest in the famous work of Geoffrey Chaucer, one of the greatest poet of the Middle Ages. While the format of this novel is a narrative prose rather than the accentual syllabic meter using a five-stress line format used by Chaucer, it has other distinctions that evolved during the writing process. Originally intended to be written with individual stories, as Chaucer had penned, the final book resulted in a single story. Yet, the author's intent was only strengthened by using this approach.

Chaucer's tales are legendary and each story reflected something intrinsic about the character who told it. It also conveyed sentiments at the time about society and the way classes interacted and viewed one another. In this book, there are similarities, yet the book conveys the ability —and the hope — that differences in class, age, gender, and other demographics can still result in a coalescence of ideas into a single, uninterrupted narrative. The writer leaves the interpretation of the result to the ultimate judgment of the reader.

Following citation: Wikipedia

Geoffrey Chaucer; (c. 1343 – 25 October 1400), known as the Father of English literature, is widely considered the greatest English poet of the Middle Ages. He was the first poet to be buried in Poets' Corner of Westminster Abbey.

While he achieved fame during his lifetime as an author, philosopher, and astronomer. He is best known today for *The Canterbury Tales*.

Chaucer's work was crucial in legitimizing the literary use of the Middle English vernacular at a time when the dominant literary languages in England were French and Latin.

Waterbury Tales

Waterbury Tales
Three-Word Stories: One Tale

Prologue

I t was an unlikely gathering, but it happened just the same. I am compelled to tell this story as I witnessed it all those many years ago. As if it were a vivid dream, I recall traveling to a village in a far-off corner of England. Its name is Waterbury, a small town, not much larger than others that surrounded it.

All of us had purchased tickets to this town using a coach line that was scheduled for discontinuance. Few people traveled between metropolitan areas by bus anymore, and as this was one of the last trips to be taken, the bus was filled to capacity. In total, there were thirty-six, crimson seats – all stitched with coarse, yellow thread and all high-backed and heavily padded. I had always feared flying -- scared that a winged monkey might appear on the outside, staring in at me with red eyes and an evil grin.

So, I usually rode the bus from place to place, planning well in advance for the two-to-six-hour journey that would deposit me where an airplane would have dropped me several hours earlier. However, I thought the benefits would be getting to meet other people and see the small towns that made up the great isle of Britain – my home and one I had always loved and admired.

Unfortunately, most of these sentiments were dashed after my first bus trip when I learned that the coach rarely used secondary A-roads, preferring the major motorways or M-roads instead. On the M-roads, one never passed through a small town; rather, the coach would only pass through the congested petrol depots with their M&S Foods, KFC, or McDonald's for entertainment.

However, this time, I found an off-the-beaten-path trip that took me along the highways and byways of England's countryside - mostly A-roads but also several B-roads. I was excited to see what new experiences awaited me, but it soon became apparent that this would be much more of an adventure than I ever imagined.

*****

Waterbury Tales

Waterbury Tales

CH 1 The Long Journey Begins

It was the 10:15 bus that I had booked out of my home city. My ticket read: *Blue Egret Bus Lines, A151, departing Friday, April 3, at 10:15, arriving at 16:30.* And, true to form, I got there an hour early at 9:15 just to be sure I got a good seat. I had always been that way - overachieving in everything I tried. I never liked to be late or to miss the opportunity to get the best of whatever was being offered.

The coach line began filling the bus at ten o'clock. The driver opened each of the compartments under the monstrous vehicle to let passengers stuff their overpacked suitcases below to make room for their other, smaller, but no less annoying, other suitcases in the cabin with them. Usually, they ended up cramming them in the overhead or under the seat in front of them. In this case, since there were a few extra seats available, the early-birds plopped their extra gear in the seat next to them so no one else could bother them.

The departure time of 10:15 came and went, and still more passengers showed up to get onboard. Finally, fifteen minutes later, the driver pulled the large, single door closed and slammed his foot down to engage the accelerator.

"Welcome to bus A151. This bus will be stopping at the following towns, Sheffield, Chesterfield, ..." began the driver. After listing them, he continued, "... and as you know, it will take us over six hours to reach our final destination, Waterbury. This will be the final voyage of this coach on this route, as we will no longer be servicing these towns. However, we do appreciate your business. Now, sit back and relax. We have a lot of driving ahead of us."

I tucked my small satchel below the seat in front of me and pushed the smooth, chrome button on my chair, letting the headrest slide effortlessly back and into place to get a little rest.

"Do you mind!" came the shrieking voice from behind me.

I peered between the seats and saw an older man with a gnarled face and unsympathetic brow staring angrily back at me.

"Sorry," I said, quickly adjusting my seat up so as not to disturb him anymore.

13

It was an hour to our first stop, and when we pulled into the rest area most of the twenty-three on board got off to stretch or use the bathroom. There was a BP petrol station, a KFC and the M&S Foods store, a convenience shop, so I got off just to get a cup of badly-needed Joe. It took longer than expected, as the line was long and there was only one attendant behind the counter servicing everyone. When I finally reached the counter, the coach driver called out. "Alright, everyone back on the bus. I'm leavin' in three."

Hopeful he wouldn't leave me, I plunked down my pound-fifty and got my short, black coffee. I was the last one back on the bus, and the driver huffed as I trudged up the three worn steps to find my seat. Slamming the door behind me, the driver released the brake and headed out, the bus jerking until it reached its cruising speed.

The scenery was pastoral and peaceful, just as I remembered. It had been years since I had ventured outside of Manchester, and I thought it would do me good to get away. There was no real purpose to my trip, other than to decompress and clear my mind of all the stresses that had built-up during the week -- hell, during the previous year.

But as the countryside continued to churn past and the morning hours grew long, I began to awaken from my semi-slumbering state. I sat toward the back of the coach -- in fact, the very back. There, I hoped not to be bothered by others walking past me and disturbing my tranquility. Although I had initially planned to mingle amongst the patrons, my thoughts changed once I got on board. Solitude overcame my desire to socialize.

Yet, once awakened, I became aware of my surroundings. Glancing around, I noticed that the group on the bus was quite eclectic - one I never could have imagined gathering in one place. In front of me were a shopkeeper and his wife. To my left, two young sisters who seemed to be on their phones the entire time - giggling and texting. There were others too -- all taking the same journey, including a photographer, a doctor, a journalist, a construction worker, an attorney, an author, a government worker, a banker, a lorry driver, an actor, a small business owner, a physicist, a soldier, an engineer, a professor, a minister, and an architect. In addition, there was an old man, an old woman, a set of elderly ladies and a single-mother with two young girls. You're probably wondering how I know all this. But as events unfolded, I got to know each of them much more.

However, at this point, nothing troubled me as we cruised through the bucolic woods between Manchester and Sheffield and then on southward through Chesterfield and Loughborough. There were several stops along the way, and although a few of the passengers disembarked here and there, most stayed on - bound for the ultimate destination of Waterbury. Of those departing us at Coventry and Birmingham, were the woman with the two young girls, the old man and the set of older ladies, whom I believed to be sisters.

It was now 11:45 in the morning, and the sun was cresting in the sky and already falling toward the western horizon. The terrain was becoming more rugged and the rocky landscape of the southwest territory, as I called it, was becoming more apparent. It was about this time that all of us heard a distinctive *pop*. It was a metallic-kind of sound, like something had exploded under the hood. And soon, smoke began pouring out of the front bonnet, billowing up into the sky like we were having a good-ole-fashion American barbeque. Rotating the steering wheel to the left, the driver pulled the bus off onto the shoulder as far as he could.

"Must be a flat," he announced, having no idea what was wrong but still tipping his cap back on his head. "I'll go check. It may only take a moment."

We all knew it was something more serious than a flat tire, but heck, we figured the driver probably knew more about it than we did. He'd been doing it for many years, after all.

Patiently, we waited. At first, the delay didn't bother us, but as the minutes ticked on, we became more irritated. Finally, after twenty minutes or so, the lawyer in the group got up and stormed off the bus to confront the driver. We could only hear bits and pieces of words exchanged, but they weren't pleasant. The barrister was hot, and became even more irritated after being told that we were stuck there for a while. She came back on the bus cursing.

"What's going on?" the banker asked, watching her stomp her heels as she walked back down the aisle.

"We have a blown engine," said the barrister. "The driver has no idea how long it will take to get someone here to pick us up. He's not getting any reception with his cell phone where we are. There doesn't seem to be any cell tower nearby."

Other people on the bus then pulled out their own cell phones and began trying to call, but as I watched, all of them soon began shaking their heads.

"I'm not getting anything," said one.

"Neither am I," said another.

"We must be in a valley right here," said a third. "We may have to walk a bit until we catch a signal."

"Okay, then," said the barrister. "Who's going?"

Everyone looked at each other expecting someone else to do the heavy lifting, but no one volunteered.

It was then that the bus driver came back onboard, sweaty and hot. "I have some bad news," he said.

"We already know," said the banker. "She already told us," he added, pointing at the attorney.

"Oh," answered the driver, sheepishly. "Well then, all I can say is we have to wait until someone drives by. Hopefully, we can catch their attention and have them call for us once they get a few kilometers up the road and can get some reception. Of all the places along this route, this is the only one where we can't catch a cell tower."

"How far away is the next cell tower?" asked the attorney, impatiently.

"I think it's about ten kilometers from here in either direction, plus or minus," said the driver.

"Plus or minus what?" asked the banker.

"Plus or minus another ... ten," said the driver, wincing as he mouthed the words.

Everyone groaned. Twenty kilometers would take someone hours to reach.

"I guess we wait, then," said the banker.

"This is not a heavily traveled road, but I expect someone to be driving by sometime soon," said the driver.

However, the minutes passed, and then the hours. Still no one came. It was odd – no more like bizarre. Everyone understood that we were on a country road, but even country roads had traffic. Strangely, this one had none.

As night drew closer, everyone became more restless. Finally, the discomfort was broken by the sound of an approaching car, and the faint beam of the headlights gradually bathed more and more of the coach in their luminescence. It was speeding toward us at a fast clip, and it was almost past us before the driver could jump out and began waving it down. He put his hands high over his head and stood near the middle of the road to ensure he would be seen.

I looked out my scratched-up window, glancing down onto the pavement below where the driver was frantically trying to make contact with the car. The light from the vehicle splashed onto his face, reflecting a smile he graciously hoped would gain some attention from a good Samaritan.

But what I recall now that seemed so peculiar was that the sound of the car didn't drop in tone; it didn't seem to be slowing at all. The next sound I heard was a sickening *thump*. I looked back and saw the bus driver's body stretched out in the roadway, lifeless and dark. The car that hit him never stopped, continuing on as if nothing had happened.

We all rushed out of the bus to see what had happened. The doctor on board immediately stooped next to the body to check the driver's pulse and his pupils.

It was an anxious few minutes before she announced, "He's alive, but barely." She then looked over his extremities checking for broken bones and for internal hemorrhaging. "He's got a broken tibia and probably broken ribs, and he may be bleeding inside. I can splint his broken leg, but I'm worried about the internal bleeding – possibly his spleen. If we can't get him to a hospital, he may not make it."

Three of us helped the doctor immobilize him, moving him off to the side of the road. The doctor set about splinting the leg and taping his ribs, but there wasn't much more we could do except wait for the next set of headlights and hope those were owned by someone more humane than the last one.

It was now six o'clock and as darkness blanketed the trees and roadway, the chill of fall also descended upon us. Someone had an extra blanket in her luggage, and we covered the bus driver to keep him warm until we got our next opportunity for freedom. But that chance would not come for a while.

Two more hours passed, and as the cold began to grip our bodies, so too did our dour and negative mood. Expectedly, the complaining only grew worse. The attorney was beyond infuriated; the banker overly inconvenienced; the accountant simply bored; and the rest becoming increasingly annoyed. The construction worker wished only to get home to his family but made the mistake of mouthing off to the professor about how his job was the hardest of anyone's, including the professor's. The professor, a teacher of social science, replied that his job was far worse than anyone else's. "After all," he replied, "I must tolerate the addle-brains of the youth or people like you who think they know so much more than anyone else."

The two almost came to blows before the journalist broke up the fight. "Men, now, now," he said, stepping in between them. "There's no reason to make this trip any worse than it already is. Neither of you understands what's at stake with this nation. It takes someone like a journalist to fight for the values we all hold dear to us. So, you need to calm own!"

"What?" screeched the government bureaucrat, sitting close by. "What makes you the *keeper* of what is right and pure?"

I remember distinctly that this was a turning point. This was when the entire bus started to let go – when everyone was at each other's throats, arguing, cursing, yelling, and on the verge of outright fisticuffs. As for me, I vowed to stay out of it. After all, I was trying to find peace within myself, and I felt that intervening would have been the worst thing I could have done.

But my intervention wasn't necessary after all. What I recall happening next was not unusual or extraordinary at all; yet, in hindsight, it was the most remarkable thing that ever happened to me - to us -- in our entire lives.

CH 2 Sword Beach

It was shortly after the altercation in the bus that all of us heard the doctor's voice outside. "Hello?" she called out, her voice nervous and trembling.

Then, we heard another voice, but it wasn't the bus driver's.

"Yes, hello," a man's voice said, approaching the doctor who was monitoring the driver's condition.

Concerned, I got off the coach to see who it was and make sure she was safe. Standing in front of the doctor and the driver was a tall man wearing blue jeans, a dark gray hoodie with Notre Dame University written in blue and metallic gold on the front, well-worn brown hiking boots, and a black backpack. Under the backpack was a dirty, amber roll for a sleeping bag with large, plastic bottles of water tucked neatly in on the other side. As for the man, he had long hair, down to his shoulders - auburn brown in fact. His complexion was rather dark - Middle Eastern, I believe. When he turned around, I was struck by his piercing blue-green eyes - unusual for someone from the Middle East, but I promise, that's the color they were. His facial features were angular and handsome - his eyes deep-set, and his nose straight and noble. He wore an unkempt beard, but he didn't seem threatening or out-of-sorts. Instead, there was a quiet, peacefulness about him that gave me unusual calm.

The man looked over at me as I jumped down from the bus, and he smiled. "Hi, I'm Manny," he said, reaching out his hand. We shook, but he quickly went back to the doctor, taking off his backpack and kneeling next to the driver. "What' wrong with him?" he asked with sincere concern.

"Someone hit him with their car," said the doctor. "He's got internal bleeding. We need to get him to a hospital. Does your phone work out here?"

The man shook his head. "No, I'm afraid it doesn't. I didn't even bring it with me. I know the towers out here are unreliable. There isn't another good one for nearly thirty kilometers. I've been hiking out this way for the better part of a week. You're the first people I've come across."

"What?" asked the doctor, saddened by the news. "How could that be? We're not that far from a nearby town, are we?"

The man shook his head. "Yeah, I know. It's strange. In almost any other part of England you would be within two kilometers of civilization. Yet, right here, somehow, we're a long way away." Looking down at the suffering driver, the man asked, "Is there anything I can do?"

"Nothing anyone of us can do right now. We just need a hospital."

The man nodded before he rose. I followed him back to the bus where he climbed the three, black treads and stood in the center aisle.

"Hi, I'm Immanuel, but you can call me Manny," he said, smiling and giving a small wave. "How is everyone doing?"

As expected, the most disgruntled let loose with a barrage of curses and complaints about the entire episode.

"... and we've been sitting here for hours!" said the attorney, fuming. "I've got a court case in the morning. I can't be here twiddling my thumbs while this company figures out how to run a bus line. I'm going to sue the hell out of them when I get back to Manchester."

The banker was next to jump in. "Yeah, and I had a meeting tonight that I missed. The company's going to hear from my lawyers too."

As the others began to chime-in, the poor hiker stood and passively listened, not uttering a sound, as if he were the corporate representative who had come only to hear their grievances.

"*Whoa, whoa!*" the man began, eventually putting his hands out to silence them. "I'm not here to listen to your complaints. Instead, I thought I might be able to help you pass the time – you know, until someone does come who can get you out of this mess. What do you say?"

"No!" said the lawyer. "I don't want to *pass the time.* I want *out* of here, and I want out right now!"

"I see," said the man. "Well, I'm going to help the others anyway. So, who here wants to play a little game?"

No one raised their hand. No one was in a mood to play a game. Even I thought it was silly to propose a game of all things. We were tired, cranky and just wanted out of this mess – not to engage in some sort of *game.*

"I see," said the hiker. "I guess I have a tough crowd tonight. Well, that's not stopped me before. You see, I'm a counselor. I help people when they become lost and can't find their way; so, this is perfect for me. This is what I do, you see."

"But this isn't what you *should* do," said the actor. "I should know. I entertain people for a living. I know when it's the right time and place to entertain people, and now is *not* the time."

"Perhaps you're right," answered the man. "There is a time and a place for everything in life, and I think the time and place for counseling is right here and right now. So, who's with me?"

Still no one raised their hand -- except me. I thought, *why not? Even though I didn't feel like it either, I felt somehow that we could all use it.*

"Ah, very good," said the man, letting me pass by him and return to my seat at the back of the bus. "And what is your name, my good man?"

"I'm Paul," I said, "Paul Tarsus."

"Good. Very good," said Manny. "Well, Paul, I have some small note papers I would like you to distribute to everyone here on the bus. I also have a few pens. Would you do that?"

"Sure," I said.

He gave me the paper and pens, and I was able to hand one of each to everyone on the bus. While I was doing that, he continued his session.

"What I want each of you to do is list three things on that piece of paper. Just write them down and then fold it up. We'll collect them and I'll put them in my brown, sock hat right here."

"I'm not doing anything so stupid," said the attorney, throwing her paper down on the floor in front of her. "This is childish."

The banker did the same, only without saying a word. A few others also wadded up their papers and let them fall to the floor in front of them.

"That's sad," said the man. "I mean, really. What do you have to lose? Do you have anything else to do right now other than complain? All I'm asking is for you to list three things on a tiny piece of paper."

"What kind of things?" asked the accountant. "Are they supposed to be nouns, verbs, adjectives, what?"

"It's up to you. List anything you want," said Manny.

Intrigued, many of us began thinking and then putting down one or two things on the paper. Several seemed stumped by the simple exercise, but others quickly scribbled something and then held up their hands, ready to deposit their wonderful and thoughtful literary pieces into the hiker's hat.

"Everyone finished?" he asked finally. He began walking down the aisle taking the slips, folding them and putting them into his hat.

From what I could tell about two-thirds of the people put a folded square into the hat. Then, they all looked on curiously as the man shook the hat to mix up the pieces inside. "I'll get these good and jumbled before we start," he said.

"Start what?" asked the older lady, sitting in the front row on the right side of the coach, just behind the driver.

"Those who put in a piece of paper will draw one out. If it's the one you put in, then put it back and draw another," he instructed.

"What are we supposed to do with it?" I asked him.

"I'll tell you after someone draws the first piece," he answered. "Now, who wants to be first?"

Of course, no one volunteered, so once again I raised my hand. "I'll go," I said, shaking my head at the lack of participation. "I'm not afraid. Who knows, this could be fun!"

Manny made his way to the back of the bus and held out the sock hat. "Now, just pick one piece. If it's the one you put in, you must put it back and choose another."

I closed my eyes and reached into his hat. Pulling out a folded, somewhat crumpled, piece of paper, I could tell immediately that it wasn't the one I had put in. Carefully, I unfolded it and read the words silently to myself.

"Read the three words on the paper to all of us," said the man.

I looked again at the words and read them aloud. They were foreign to me, but I would come to understand them better within the next few minutes: "*War*, *wife*, *mission*," I said, confused with the intent.

"Good," Manny answered, "now, I want you to tell us a tale – a story -- including those three words. You can't just throw them into your story as an afterthought. They must be part of the essence and fabric of the story. After you've finished, we'll get the rest of the bus to give you a score from one to five -- one being abysmal and five being amazing. Of course, no one wants to be on the abysmal side, now do we."

Everyone groaned. "Are you kidding?" said the attorney. "This is stupid." Several others grumbled as well.

"That's fine," said the man. "Then maybe we'll dispense on the scores. We'll just enjoy the stories. But in the end, maybe we'll vote on who had the best one. How's that? Now, Paul, we'll give you a few minutes to gather your thoughts, and then you can begin. Your story should be no more than about five minutes. If you're not finished within that time. the bus can decide on whether to give you more time to finish or cut you off. Does everyone understand? … Good. Okay, so you're up!" he exclaimed, pointing at me.

I thought long and hard about a story that might contain those words. I assumed the slip had come from the man in uniform on the bus. If only I could have talked to him to find out what he was thinking when he wrote them down. I didn't know anything about him or what experiences he might have been through. All of that would have made things a lot easier. So, I struggled for words. Yet, finally, something came to me.

"Okay," I said after more than five minutes. I took a deep breath and stood at the back of the coach, addressing everyone in front of me. "It all started in the fall of 1939. I was sitting on a stool in Henry's Pub with some of my mates drinking a pint and listening to the radio as our prime minister came on to the airwaves. We had been in the place for a few hours, sucking down our third round, when I distinctly remember Churchill saying 'This morning the British ambassador in Berlin handed the German government a final note stating that unless we heard from their government by eleven o'clock London time that the Third Reich was prepared at once to withdraw their troops from Poland, a state of war would exist between us.' I had glanced up at the clock and realized that it was well into the afternoon at that point, and a cold shock came over me.

23

Our prime minister went on to state that he had received no such word. We all knew then, that we were at war."

"Within three months, many of my friends had enlisted even though they were older than the twenty-to-twenty-two conscription requirement enacted, but I held out – thinking the war would all be over quickly and my involvement wouldn't be necessary. But by the fall, I too had no choice. Parliament enacted conscription laws that went all the way up to age forty-one. So, there I was, standing in an army uniform by the end of 1939.

"I wasn't involved in the Dunkirk episode, but after the forced evacuation of British troops from those beaches in 1940 it became clear that this would become a war for national survival. In fact, my first battlefield experience was a day I will remember forever - June 6, 1944. Indeed, D-day would be remembered forever, but only by those of us who survived it.

"While the Americans landed on Omaha and Utah beaches, we Brits took the sands at Gold and Sword. Mine was Sword. Wearing gray fatigues, a helmet and carrying a Lee Enfield rifle, I remember crouching inside an amphibious landing craft – what we called an LCI for landing craft infantry. We were bounced around in the heavy seas like we were in the rear car of a rollercoaster. There were artillery shots landing in the water all around us, but luckily none hit their mark.

"When we got close to shore, the bow of the LCI suddenly dropped open, and we were expected to jump off and wade in toward the beach. I watched in horror as the first line of men leaped from the end, but we were too far out. They sank to the bottom like rocks, drowning within minutes. The rest stood back and waited until we got closer, but by that time we were so close to the beach that we caught the strafing from German machine gun nests above us. The first three rows of men in the front of the craft died instantly. It was sickening to watch as they fell into the sea and floated like bobbers on a fishing line. Unwilling to die without a fight, the rest of us jumped into the fomenting waters and did what we could to swim to shore with twenty kilos strapped to our backs.

"But once on shore, we found no mercy. Bullets started flying over my head almost from the moment I planted my boots in the sand. To the right of me and to the left, I saw friends' heads blown off and arms and legs shredded into what looked like strands of spaghetti. Yet, there was only one way I could make it out alive - continue fighting and moving forward, an inch at a time.

"After what seemed like hours, we made it to the German bunkers, and as the bullets streamed out of the tiny slits that had been cut into the concrete slab, I grabbed a hand grenade from my belt. Pulling the pin, I cooked-off two seconds before stuffing it down and inside the bunker. It blew almost immediately, sending smoke and shrapnel everywhere inside. The chatter of the machine gun suddenly grew silent.

"But this was only the start of our journey. Our orders were to go beyond the beach heads and capture as much territory as we could while we had the element of surprise on our side. So, we pressed on to Ouistreham, a small town along Sword beach. The first part of our mission was to take that small town -- one that had been overrun by the Germans four years earlier. Although a town of only fifteen hundred, it was still a strategic stronghold and critical to capturing others along that road. Ultimately, our goal was to free the country and liberate Paris. Those goals would be achieved, but not without sacrifice.

"That night, I hunkered-down in my trench. All I could think about were my brother and his wife and kids. He was out there someplace too, but I didn't know where. He had come across in the same armada to Noland T.dy that day but on a different boat. We were assigned to different corps units, and so we had separate missions. I just prayed he had survived the day.

"The next morning, we found ourselves pounded by enemy fire. The bombs fell line rain around us, and we waited for air support to chase the Me109 fighters away. We were several clicks from Ouistreham and a long way from Caen. Hell, even one kilometer seemed impossible when being bombed, strafed and shot at. But, this was only the beginning. Things would only get more interesting."

I smiled and sat down. I had told the story, and had used the three words as I was told. Now it was someone else's turn to take the torch, I thought.

"A *very* good start," said Manny, smiling at me. Then he glanced down at his hat and the other pieces of paper nestled inside. "So, who wants to be next?"

No one else raised their hand, so Manny waited. Still nothing. Finally, he walked over to one of the two young girls sitting together next to me. "What's your name?" he asked one of them.

"I'm Theresa," she answered. She was only in her early twenties, and looked very much like the girl sitting next to her. Both had round faces and hair cut short on the sides but long and flopped-over on top. As for the color, it was more of a

25

chocolate cherry tone with amethyst highlights, I'd say. Each had numerous ear piercings, but one had many more in one ear which resembled a sequin-studded, Hollywood runway dress. Their eyes dark with mascara and eyeliner, they only differed by what they wore. One had a short, denim skirt with knee-length socks pulled up to her thighs and a heavy, brown suede Samet with a raw wool collar. The other had torn jeans and open-toed sandals. Her navy, fleece Samet covered her light gray, V-neck sweater which she wore without a necklace. It was this latter girl whom Manny had approached to carry the story.

"Theresa, glad to know you. Are you a student?"

"Yeah. I'm with my sister, here."

"Going home, I take it?"

"Yeah?" she answered, this time surprised at the accuracy of Manny's presumptions.

"Well, that's nice. Mum and dad, I'm sure, will be happy to see both of you. Now, would you be so kind as to reach into the hat and pull out a paper?"

The girl looked at Manny suspiciously, but then reluctantly extended her arm and plunged her fingers into the cap, pulling out a slip.

"What does it say?" asked Manny.

Theresa opened the paper and read its contents: "*Rules*, *French fries*, and *telephone*," she said. "That shouldn't be too hard to make a story out of that."

"You're right, but I'm going to change the rules a bit," said Manny. "I liked Paul's story so much, I want to continue it. So, you'll need to weave those three words together into a story that begins where his left off."

Theresa's mood instantly changed. "Hell no!" she said, throwing the paper on the floor of the bus. "You can't just change the rules on us like that. You can't!"

Manny nodded. "You're right. That was unfair. So, I'll put it to a vote of the rest of the bus. Do you want to continue Paul's story?"

"Yes!" most cried out with nodding heads.

"That's not right!" Theresa snapped back. "I won't do it!"

"What if I give you a coach?"

Theresa just stared at him waiting for what he would say next.

Manny continued. "I'll make it even easier for you. You can ask Paul to help you. In fact, anyone can ask the previous storyteller to help you. Would that work?"

I looked over at the young woman who returned my glance immediately. She was shaking her head no, while I was nodding mine yes.

"Okay, let's make it more interesting, then," said Manny. He reached into his pocket and pulled out a one-hundred-pound note and placed it on the seat of the driver. "Whoever tells the best segment of this story -- as voted by a majority of people on this bus -- wins the money. What do you say to that?"

"I'm in!" Theresa shouted suddenly.

"Now, no one can vote for their own story," said Manny, "but the one who gets the most votes will win. And if a person helps, they get half."

"It's a deal," I said, smiling and taking up the challenge with Theresa.

There were those like the banker and some others who were less than impressed by the winnings offered, but their interest perked-up a bit more than it had before. The evening was about to get more interesting.

*****

CH 3 The Farmer and His Wife

I moved over to where Theresa was sitting, and together we talked about how she could move the story forward with those three clues. When she was comfortable, she began.

"So," she started, trying to remember the three words, "we began marching east toward Caen. Our platoon ..." she paused and looked at me to make sure she was using the right word, "... was taking the forward position as we walked, I mean marched, toward that other town -- *Oust*-something."

I softly whispered it to her. "Ouistreham," I said.

"Yeah, Ouistreham," she repeated. "So, we had our rules, you know. The general told us what we needed to do. It was, like, our mission, I guess. But, it was a long way to this town, and it wasn't easy to get there. The road was muddy and filled with ruts and stuff from the tanks. It had rained only a few days before, and it was starting to rain again, as the clouds and winds began to pick-up."

I smiled. I could tell Theresa was beginning to enjoy herself. She was getting more comfortable, just relaxing and letting the story come to her.

"Yeah, so, we were all trudging along this road, and the pack on my back was killing me. It was so heavy, I wasn't sure how I was going to make it to the town, but since my leader … my commander … said we had to fight the Germans and take it back, I kept going, you know.

"It was about then when we came to this intersection, but there weren't any road signs to tell us what is what. We weren't sure which direction to go in. All the fields around us looked the same, and the platoon leader -- the lieutenant?" she said, again looking at me, "wasn't sure either. I checked my pockets and for some reason I hadn't brought my cell phone, so we couldn't call anyone for help."

At this, most in the bus started laughing.

"What's wrong?" she asked. "What did I say?"

"You're doing great, Theresa. Keep going. It's really wonderful," said Manny, encouraging her.

"Well, so we couldn't telephone anyone for directions. But there was a farm house off in the distance, so we started moving toward that. It was small - a two-story, brown-bricked house with two chimneys - one on either end. Not far away was the barn, also not big. It was old and rather dilapidated. Certainly, it hadn't been painted in a long time.

"The lieutenant stopped us outside the house, putting up his fist. He went to the door, holding his pistol, just in case there were Germans inside. There, he knocked on the door and said, 'Hello?' then he added in bad French *'Bon jour?'* but, his English accent made sure that anyone inside would know he wasn't from their country.

"But suddenly, the white front door to the house opened, and the owner stood there holding a scary-looking shotgun. He was an older guy, probably in his early sixties, with a short, wispy mustache and piercing blue eyes. He answered in French, even though we didn't know what he was saying. However, there was somebody in our platoon who knew French and asked the lieutenant if he could talk to the man.

"He was my good friend, Luke. He had studied French in high school, so he knew more than the rest of us. He walked up to the front porch and said in French, something like *Hi, we're from England and we're here to free your country'* – or something like that anyway. Thank God, the old man smiled and put down his gun. He called to his wife and both came out and hugged the lieutenant and my friend. The next thing we knew, they invited all of us to come in and join them for supper.

"Boy, I was sure hungry too. And the old woman there cooked us a feast for sore eyes. We had been living off army food … rations … for days, even before we'd gotten on the boat for Noland T.dy, and having a good home-cooked meal was awesome! She cooked a beef roast, a mix of cooked turnips and carrots and a big bowl of French fries. The fries were mounded high on the plate too. They were the best fries I had ever eaten in my life -- better even than McDonald's."

Again, the group laughed.

"Well, almost better than McDonald's," said Theresa, smiling. "But they were really good. Then, after dinner we sat in their living room, which was really small, and we talked about what life was like there while the German's had taken over things."

Theresa looked over at Manny and stopped. "I think that's it. That's all I can think of," she said, sitting back down in her bus seat.

"Well, I'm impressed," said Manny. "You did great. So, who's next? Where does this story go from here?"

Again, no one raised his or her hand. So, Manny said. "Okay, then what we'll do is this. The last person to tell the story will pick the next person to tell the story. So, Theresa, who is next?"

Theresa smiled and began looking around the bus. People began putting their heads down, trying to avoid eye contact. Her sister was especially afraid of being picked, since it would be just like Theresa to pick her. However, Theresa's eyes moved elsewhere within the bus and fixed on someone farther up the rows. "That man there," she said pointing. "He should be next."

At first the man looked at her blankly, glancing behind him as though she were pointing to someone else. However, when it was clear to whom she was pointing, he began shaking his head. "No, I'm afraid not," he said, putting up his hands. It was the banker who had thrown the paper down on the floor, along with the attorney and a few others.

The man was large, requiring all of his own seat and part of one next to him to seat himself comfortably. Although not dressed in a three-piece, gray, pin-striped suit, he did wear a long-sleeved, blue shirt and red-striped tie over which he had layered a navy, cardigan vest. His girth was extraordinary, as were the triple chins that he sported. His neck was so large it nearly disappeared – his head extending almost directly onto his shoulders. With a trimmed, gray beard, he had a head that was covered only on the sides by patches of gray that navigated around his protruding ears. Yet, he had an equal amount of gray hairs poking out of his ears themselves and framing the front of his face as a unibrow that spanned the tops of both his eyes.

"You're up," said Manny, not letting him off the hook. "What's your name?" Manny asked.

"I'm Charley," the man said, clearly put-out.

"And tell us a little about yourself, Charlie," asked Manny.

"Well, I work for a bank in Manchester. I'm just on my way to see my daughter who lives in Waterbury."

"And do you have family in Manchester?"

"Not now. My wife passed last year. My daughter and her family have been asking that I move down to live with them, but I'm only three years from retirement, so I'm staying in Manchester for now."

"Charlie, I'm sorry for your loss. It's difficult to live alone, I'm sure."

"Yes, it's been a difficult time," said Charlie, suddenly softening.

"Hey, if you don't want to tell us a story, that's okay. We'll give you a pass if you like."

It was as if the magic words had been spoken, and given the choice instead of a mandate, the banker had a change in heart and tone.

"No, I'll give it a try," he said, seeming to enjoy the challenge. He picked up the paper he had tossed on the floor and filled it out. "So, where's the hat?"

Manny produced the hat, and Charley pulled out his piece of paper and then dropped inside the one he had prepared. He unfolded the one he'd chosen and read the results. "*Starving*, *business*, *worry*."

"Do you need help?" Manny asked.

Charley shook his head. "No, I think I got this," he answered.

*****

CH 4 Fertilizing the Trees

"We continued talking well into the night," Charlie began, his voice high-pitched and strained. Yet, the more he spoke the more warmth permeated his dialog - a sincerity that made it almost believable. "The farmer told us about how badly the Germans had treated them during those years under captivity. He said they had taken over his business and stolen much of the money he had saved for his family to live on. Every year, the Nazis had demanded he give the Fuhrer fifty percent of what he made. Having no choice, he complied, but it left him hardly enough to live on. In fact, he told us many of his animals had starved to death because he wasn't able to feed them. All he and his wife could do was worry, and it seemed they both began worrying more and more each day. Soon, he thought, his wife and he wouldn't have enough to live on.

"Things grew worse until one day, the farmer said he had had enough. When the Gestapo had come to collect their fifty percent, he had told them he didn't have it. He said he was broke, which he was, and he couldn't pay them anything. He understood the ramifications of what he was saying, but things had grown so bad that they had nothing else to lose.

"'I see,' the Nazi officer had said, gruffly. 'So, you're telling me you have nothing to give the Fuhrer?' The farmer said he had only nodded, unable to speak another word and waited for the bullet to come. 'Well, I guess we'll have to take our cut in some other way then,' the German had said. Then, the Gestapo agent and his men left.

"The farmer said he had looked at his wife with a puzzled expression and she had done the same back to him. 'I guess it could have been worse,' the farmer had said to his wife, shrugging.

"It was only a few minutes later when the farmer heard the sickening sound of gunfire coming from behind his barn. He had rushed outside to see what was happening when he saw the Germans all standing with their pistols raised, shooting down every last one of his farm animals. They all lay dead in the pasture behind the house. "'That should teach you not to short-change the Fuhrer.' the German officer had said with an evil stare.

"My mates and I sat there in the farmer's living room speechless – unable to move. I remember glancing over at the lieutenant and seeing the white, pallid face as if he were shocked by the story. Then, I looked to Luke who had been translating everything. "Are you sure that's what he said?" I had asked. My friend only nodded grimly.

"'So, then what happened?' the lieutenant had asked, as mesmerized by the farmer's story as I was.

"The farmer began choking up, so it was his wife who put her hand on his and continued the tale. 'They left,' she added. 'But that wasn't the end of things. You see, they were back in another month, except this time it was just one of the Germans, not the entire mob. Again, he demanded his fifty percent and said he wasn't leaving until we gave it to him.'

"'But since you didn't have anything left to give him, what did you do?' asked Luke.

"'He didn't leave,' said the farmer, neither smiling nor frowning.

"'I don't understand,' said Luke. 'What do you mean, he didn't leave?'"

"The farmer merely nodded his head toward the back of the house. He didn't say anything more. It was his wife who clarified, saying, 'He will be fertilizing our trees in the back for some time.'"

Charlie paused, unsure at first whether he had anything more to add to the story or whether to leave it there. Pleased with himself, he just nodded and sat down. It was a poignant ending, and he was content to leave it that way.

"*Wow*," said Manny, "I wasn't expecting that. *Very good*, Charlie. Very good. Okay, so who would you like to choose next?"

Charlie glanced around the bus until his eyes fell on an attractive older woman a few rows behind him. He smiled, and said, "I think you'd give us a nice story," he said.

The woman looked professional. Her hair was died a dark brunette, as her age would never have supported such a color, but it worked for her just the same. Pulled back in a bun and pinned, it made her look prim and proper, like a grandmother going to see her grandchildren. Wearing a fashionable, oversized, cutaway gray coat over a simple white blouse, she was current, yet age-appropriate. And even though age was apparent in the wrinkles in her face, she was dignified and elegant. Her earrings were plain, diamond studs and her makeup was modest with only a trace of coral lipstick.

The woman smiled at Charlie, as if he had picked her out of the crowd and asked her to dance. Without being prompted, she began. "I'm Mariam, and I'm an actor. I've been in several plays and other productions in the West End in London and have enjoyed every moment of it. This is my fall break, so I'm traveling to see my niece in Bristol." Everyone could tell instantly that she had a theatrical flair and her voice carried through the bus like an orator in a Greek tragedy. "Now, the hat please," she beamed, relishing the limelight.

Manny produced the hat, and she extracted a piece of paper. She then unfurled it and read the contents. However, it was then that I noticed her grimace, as though she'd eaten a sour piece of orange. "Is it possible to choose another?" she asked, starting to put the paper back.

"No, I'm afraid you must use the paper you've chosen," said Manny.

Mariam looked slightly put-out, but she merely said, "Fine," as she wadded up the small sheet.

"My words are *bunnies*, *fantasy*, and *roses*. Now, where did we leave off the story?"

Charlie reminded her that it had been after the conversation about the German officer's fate.

"Oh, yes. Well, let's see. Our lieutenant – we'll call him Jack -- saw that it was getting late, and he thanked the farmer and his wife for their hospitality. We left the farmhouse and set-up our tents not far away -- just down the road in fact. I remember glancing back up toward where the farmhouse lay, thinking about the dead German officer buried up there, when I saw a bunch of bunnies scamper across the road in front of some rose bushes. The lieutenant, Jack, thought it looked like a fantasy to him." She stopped and smiled. "Well, I guess that's it," she quipped. "That's all I can come up with for these three words."

"That *sucked*!" said Theresa, who had given a great story earlier. "That was really bad! If I can get up and tell a halfway decent story, then so can you!"

"*Yeah*!" said many on the bus, disappointed with the half-hearted effort given.

"I must say that I'm less than impressed," I said from the back of the bus.

But it was Manny who took a different tack. "Mariam, I would have thought that as an actress you would have a great many stories to tell. In the fantasy world you live in on stage, that is, I would have supposed your imagination would have been sparked by at least some of the roles you played. Is that not right?"

"Well ..." she mumbled, starting to feel embarrassed.

"I assume you were - are -- very good at what you do," Manny continued. "So, as a talented actor, don't you have more to offer us than that?"

"For paying customers, it's different," she quipped, tossing a loose strand of hair behind her ear.

"Humor us," said Manny. "At least you might earn this one hundred pounds I'm offering." He held it up in his hand.

"Well, with or without the money, I'm not sure you'd understand the fine nuances of any story I would present to you," she said, trying to defend herself.

"Try us," Manny said.

She glared at him, but when he gestured with his arm for her to begin, she felt obliged.

"Alright," Mariam answered, "but buckle your seatbelts for this will be a performance like you've never seen."

*****

CH 5 Bunnies

Mariam positioned herself in the middle of the aisle and cleared her throat. She paused, collecting herself for the performance, even though I, myself, wondered whether she was waiting for a spotlight to capture her on stage before beginning.

"Our men left the farmer's house," she began. "It was getting late, as the sun had set many hours earlier. We found a small clearing off the main road – a place where we couldn't easily be seen -- and laid out our beddings.

"I was just getting settled when Luke came over and invited me to join some of the others who wanted to stay up a bit longer and talk. I wasn't so sure, but I also wasn't sure I would be able to fall asleep very easily. There were clouds overhead, but they passed quickly, allowing the reflection of the moon to blanket us with light.

"'Hey, Rex, you said your family has a farm like that farmer back there. Isn't that right? asked Luke, starting to whittle a piece of wood with his small, silver pen knife.

"Rex was our sergeant. He was a large, hulk of a man – some six feet, six and about two hundred twenty pounds. Everyone was afraid of him, even our lieutenant, who had already signed-off for the night.

"Rex looked up at Luke. I could see the confusion in his eyes. 'Why are you bringing that up?' he asked him.

"''Cause we were just at a farm house, Rex. Why do you think?' What's your farm like? Is it anything like that one?'

"'It don't have no dead Nazi in the back forty. That's for sure,' he answered, curtly.

"'We already know that,' said Luke. 'Did you have any farm animals? What were your mum and dad like?'

"Rex sighed. 'Yeah, we had lots of animals. There was sheep, goats, hogs, and horses. We had three sheepdogs, too, that kept the sheep and goats in line when they were out grazing in the fields. Dad would tell me and my brothers to go out and bring them in at night before the sun went down. We'd also have to get up at five o'clock in the morning to take care of things in the barn, feed them and let them out. Then, we'd go to class. I was the youngest three boys, and my brothers always teased me along the way. It was over two kilometers to the school house, and we trudged along the road whether it was sunny or wintery.

"'You have two brothers, then?' I asked him.

"'Yeah, me oldest brother was Nate, and then me middle brother was Timothy, although we called him *T*. Nate was a good soul, but T – he was a bit on the nasty side. He had a temper that never really got tamed.

"It was then that Rex choked up.

"'What is it?' I asked him. 'What's wrong?'

"'T's dead. The Germans killed him at Dunkirk. He was as nasty before he left on that mission as he was when we walked to school.'

"'And Nate?' Luke asked.

"Rex shook his head. 'I don't know. He's flying Spits' (referring to Spitfire fighters) – 'but I don't know where he is now. We hadn't heard anything from him before I left on D-day.'

"'What about you, Luke?' I asked. 'What's your story?'

"'Me?' he asked, 'I grew up in Birmingham. We live in a steel town – a heavy manufacturing town. People there have been working around the clock to make machines and munitions for us here in the field. My two little sisters are even working, along with my mum. They work twelve-hour days sometimes just to make sure I have bullets for my gun.'

"'That's tough,' said Will, a private sitting with us.

"'That's not the tough part. Back in March three years ago …'

"'1941?' I asked.

"'Yeah, it was during the Battle of Britain. We call it the Birmingham Blitz, when the Nazi Luftwaffe bombed the hell out of my city! They destroyed much of the town.'

"'What happened to your family?'

"'My youngest sister was killed in the raid. Mum is still in a home, recovering. She's missing her left arm and her left foot.' Luke paused a minute to control his emotions. 'Those bastards will pay for that!'

"it was quickly apparent that our conversation would be less than uplifting. Yet, it seemed most of us had an ax to grind.

"'Corporal?' asked Serg, looking at Marvin, who had also joined us, 'What about you? What's your gripe? Why do you hate the Germans?'

"Marvin was usually talkative, and this night was no exception. We worried that once started, we might not be able to shut him up. However, he too had a story worth listening to. First, he told us about his growing up. He was one of eight kids. He was the third of the eight. There were five boys and three girls. His father had left them shortly after his little brother had been stillborn. It had been hard on the whole family, but they pressed on.

"His mother had gotten a job at the local grocers to make ends meet, and even then it was barely enough to put enough food on the table. Marvin's siblings went to work too, toiling hour after hour in menial and dangerous jobs to help their mum. When the war broke out, Marvin's older brother went off to war.

"'Was it just your oldest brother who went off to war?' asked Serg. 'Or did your other older brother go off too?'

"'Peter went first,' said Marvin. 'Patrick went next. We didn't hear anything from them for quite a while. Mum and pops got a few letters from both but then they stopped from Patrick. He was the one who flew bombing raids over Europe. I remember the day when we got a knock on the door and standing in the doorway was an army major. He handed a slip of paper to pops and mumbled something to him. Pops broke down and couldn't even speak. Mum came up behind him and asked what was wrong. No one had to say anything. Mum knew.'

"'How did he die?'

"'He was on one of the bombing runs on Mannheim, Germany. His plane never made it home.'

There was silence, even though it would be a repeated story throughout the night.

"'Did your mum and pops recover from it?'

"'What choice did they have? Churchill told them to *hold a stiff upper lip*. That's what Brits do, right?'

"Serg turned to William, one of the privates who'd joined us. 'So, Will, what do you think about the Germans?'

"Will shook his head. 'I got no brothers or sisters. I do know some friends who enlisted before the mandatory. I think they're both down in Africa someplace — probably fighting in some jungle. I figure I'm better off than them.'

"'I heard they were fighting the Germans in the north — in the desert,' said Marvin. 'They would be in the hot and dry, not the wet and humid.'

"'Oh, I didn't know that,' said William.

"'And you, Collin? What's your story?' Rex asked.

"'Me?'

"'Yeah, aren't you Collin?' said Rex, poking fun at him.

"'Uh, yeah.'

"'Then, what do you have for us? Tell us about yourself,' said Marvin.

"'It's been hard,' said Collin. 'You see, even though half my family is British, the other half is German. My mum's side of the family comes from Hamburg. She's had two brothers killed in the war all ready. We can't talk about our German side or we would be shunned. Mum hasn't gone out of the house much since the war began. She's got a German accent and gets nasty stares when she talks.

"'Me parents met in Berlin about twenty-five years ago. Things were bad in Germany then, and me mum wanted to get out. She married dad in Germany, but they moved to London before having us. There are just two of us — me sister and me. She's three years older.'

"'What about your mum's parents? Are they still living in Germany?' asked Rex.

"'We don't know,' Collin said. 'We can't get any messages in or out of Germany. Mum's not heard anything, and she worries.'

"The boys talked well into the night, each sharing their personal tales. Others shared, including Percy, our lance corporal, Henry and Max, both privates, and our radio operator, Jason. Finally, the lieutenant got up from his bedroll and came over. Shaking his finger, he told us it was after three in the morning and time to hit the sack. 'We've got a long march ahead of us tomorrow. Get to sleep!'

As for me, I tossed and turned, unable to shut my eyelids during the night, and before I knew it, red and orange hues began to replace the blackness -- peaking over the distant horizon and harkening a new day.

"The scene was eerily quiet and peaceful. The birds were peeping their morning songs, while the crickets, which had been chirping all night long, had stopped their mating chants. None of us was wooed into believing that this serenity would continue through the rest of the day. We knew that at any moment, the tranquility could instantly be rocked by gunfire and violence. Indeed, the drama of the day had yet to unfold. It was only a matter of time when the Germans would roll in their army to retake what had been taken from them. Already, we had heard blasts back where we had landed on the Noland T.dy shoreline and seen greater numbers of German war planes flying overhead. To our relief, they had not yet spotted our group, but we were worried that when they did, we would relive the hell and fury we had experienced on the beachhead.

"Staying close to the tree line, we marched along the road that would take us to that Ouist- town." Here she looked at me for help, but then shook her head and continued anyway. "We were about two kilometers outside of it when we heard motorized vehicles coming our way. Jumping into the bushes, we waited. But, as soon as I landed in the bushes, I felt sharp, points of pain, as if I'd flopped down on a bed of nails. *Rose bushes* I had thought. Sure enough, there were rose thorns piercing every part of my body as if I were lying on a bed of nails. I wanted to scream, but I knew if I did I would only betray my troop. So, I bit the inside of my lip and waited.

"The line of lorries and cars," she began.

However, I did interrupt accidently -- force of habit, I suppose -- by interjecting "You mean the convoy of lorries and Willies?"

"Yes, of course," she said giving me a hardened look. "The convoy began to roll past us. I held my breath, feeling my heart thumping violently against my chest wall. At the same time, I felt something begin to drip from my lips – a saltiness that was oozing from where I'd chomped on my inner cheek. Still, I made no sound.

"We sat and watched as the convoy rolled by, the little red, Nazi flags whipping viciously from the radio aerials as if hurricane warning flags had been raised. And in some sense, they signaled just that, but it was only a calm before the storm.

"It was then that a family of bunnies ran across the road in front of one of the German lorries. The convoy -- from that lorry back - stopped. It was clear that the driver didn't want to run over the rabbits. But it seemed surreal to me that men who wanted only to kill us would be so sensitive to such tiny animals. Amazed, I watched the scene unfold, like it had been scripted by a master director. The German soldier quickly opened the door to his lorry and stood on the truck's landing. He watched the furry little creatures as they bounded across the coarse, gravel road ahead, as if this were written into the Germany army protocol.

"But within seconds, a commanding Nazi officer jumped from a jeep not far behind him. He was shouting and flailing his arms in the air. I could tell that he wasn't happy about the stop and apparently hadn't seen the army protocol for bunnies on the road. He said something to the driver, which I assume to be questioning why they had stopped. The driver merely pointed to the last of the rabbits hopping across the road in front of them.

"Immediately, the officer pulled out his pistol and began shooting at them. He killed two before the rest were able to scamper off into the brush beside the road. Then, shaking with anger, he pointed the gun at the temple of the driver, shouting *'Du Idiot! Ich sollte dich hier und jetzt erschießen!'*"

Mariam stopped and smiled. "Yes, and I know some German too," she said before continuing.

"The driver trembled and closed his eyes, awaiting his fate. But, the commander just huffed and stuffed his pistol back into his black shoulder holster. Then, he waved his hand and said, *'Lass uns gehen!* Let's go!"

"The soldiers climbed back into their lorries and roared off down the road, the dust billowing behind them. I sighed, thanking the gods for our salvation. It could have ended badly, but it didn't -- at least not then."

Mariam took her bow, expecting applause, and it was Manny who came through for her.

41

"Very nice," said Manny, initiating the clapping. "Much better. Now I understand why you are so good at what you do. Thank you for your performance. It was brilliant."

Mariam beamed and took another bow. The bus began clapping for her too -- not because her story was exceptional, but rather because that's what they thought she wanted, perhaps needed. It was odd, but as I write this account, it was true.

Then, Manny held out the brown hat again. "Who's next? Who wants to take-on the challenge of continuing our story?"

As much as many didn't want to participate, the story was getting too good and no one wanted it to end. At the same time, they weren't sure they knew where to take it.

"Come now," said Manny. "We can't let the story of our hero end here, can we?" He looked back at Mariam and asked, "Would you pick the next storyteller?"

Mariam stood up, delighted at being able to punish someone else in the group. She glanced around the bus before her eyes finally landed on a middle-aged man. He was quite unremarkable, but it is very possible that this is precisely why she chose him.

"That man there," she said pointing, her wrinkled index finger singling-out the gentlemam.

He looked surprised, presumably assuming that by glancing down and not making eye contact, she wouldn't choose him. But there was something about him that, something interesting and compelling.

Probably no more than forty-six or so, the gentleman was a large man with big hands and a big-rounded chest. Clean-shaven and clear-eyed, he looked military but his haircut suggested a more main-stream profession. The man had a head-start on a double chin, but his full, rosy cheeks and deep-set eyes framed by dark wrinkles told of a life with stresses and challenges.

Manny went to him and extended the hat. "I guess it's your turn," he said. "What is your name?"

"I'm Glen," he answered calmly.

"And what is your craft?" asked Manny.

"I'm a bobby in Waterbury. I'm going home. Been visiting family in Manchester, I have," he said.

"Well, thank you for your sevice, Glen. We know it's a tough job that you do every day and the people of England are proud to have you on the team."

"Thanks," he answered. "We do our best."

"Now, would you just reach in and ..."

Glen pulled out a sheet and read the result: "*Cast, jewelry, friendly*," he said.

"Oh, that was mine!" said Mariam, smiling with delight. "That one should be easy, I think."

But for the police officer, it was more of a challenge than he wanted to let-on. "Uh, I don't know what to do with this," he said, looking around blankly.

"Do you need help then?" asked Manny.

"Yeah, I need a lot of help, I think," he answered.

Mariam jumped up and went over to him. They began whispering back and forth until he finally nodded.

"Okay. I'll give it a go."

Manny merely gestured with his hand, and the officer began, continuing the tale.

*****

CH 6 Tea

"The sun hadn't yet gotten to its place overhead, and we had already survived a life-and-death event. If it hadn't been for the distraction of the bunnies, we might have been discovered. So, it was true that there were many who sacrificed in the war, even some rabbits now and then.

"Still, we had a job to do, and we had a long way to march. Ouistreham, ..." Glen said flawlessly before stopping and adding, "... my grandmum was from there." He then winked at me and continued, "... was only another two kilometers up the road, but it would seem like forty. The skies were clouding up - becoming overcast and rainy. We could tell from the farmlands where pools here and there dotted the fields that the countryside had gotten a lot of rain. But the cloudy, stormy skies were a blessing -- there would be less of a chance of German Messerschmitt's pounding us from the air.

"Those fields of northern France were truly beautiful, reminding me of the rolling hills near Manchester. The crops were coming up in their rows just as the farmers had planted them in the early spring forming verdant landscapes for miles around. Mostly wheat, peas, sugar beets and potatoes - all had begun popping their emerald shoots out of the ground well before then and were well on their way to a hearty harvest. The only thing stopping them would be a dry spell or errant bombs that might land on the hectares, killing every last stalk that struggled to survive.

"We patrolled the road, looking for unusual things that might tip us off as to where the Nazi's might be hiding or gathering. It was a beat we weren't used to, but we'd been trained, and we were doing our best to remember everything we'd been told.

"Even though it was early June, it was getting hot and our water supplies were running thin. I remember spotting a well next to a house not far from the road. I told the lieutenant and pointed it out, but he was reluctant. He said, 'They may not be friendly. We'll have to check them out first.'

"He sent two of us over to scout the place before risking any others. We held our Enson rifles close, ready to shoot anything that seemed threatening, but the whole damned place looked deserted. The house was peeling, and the white side boards were loose and flapping in the wind or falling off the sides. There weren't any animals around in the fields or in the barn, either. With weeds growing up everywhere, we were sure no one lived there.

"But we knocked on the door, just in case, aiming our rifles at whoever answered, but when no one answered after several minutes we thought we'd found a place to stay for the night. A few of us headed over to the well to refill our canteens when suddenly, behind us, the door opened. I swung around with my rifle, ready to pull the hair trigger on my Enson, when I saw a young woman holding an infant in her arms. She was scared.

"Crying and shaking all over, she immediately said, *'Ne nous fais pas de mal! S'il vous plaît ne nous blesse pas. C'est juste moi et mon bébé!'"*

I was very impressed that the policeman knew French, although it was far from fluent.

"'Don't hurt us! Please don't hurt us. It's just me and my baby!'" Luke added, translating for us into English. "Our French interpreter, of course, translated for Lt. Jack, and the lieutenant began walking toward her, pointing his weapon toward the ground.

"'We're not here to hurt you,' said Lt. Jack. 'We're from Britain, and we're here to help.'

"The woman sank to her knees and continued to sob. We could tell that her tears had suddenly changed from those of terror to those of relief and joy. When the lieutenant helped her up, she hugged him with her free arm and then motioned for all of us to come in.

"Quickly shutting the door behind her, she motioned for us to sit. Luke translated as she took her small child and lay it in a bassinette near the grand, stone fireplace at the far end of the room.

"'May I get you some tea?' she asked, but I wasn't sure. The next thing I knew, she left us for the kitchen, and within ten minutes I heard the water kettle whistling under a hot flame. I got up and went back to help her. As I walked in, she smiled at me and showed me where the tea bags were kept. After a few minutes, she and I brought out the hot water and tea bags and laid them all out for the men who were laughing and smoking – completely relaxed and making themselves at home.

"When her baby began whimpering, she picked it up and rocked it in her arms until it settled."

"'What is your baby's name?' I asked her.

"After it was translated, she answered, 'She's Emma, and she's only seven months old. She's my only child, and I love her dearly.'

"'And what is your name?' I asked, looking into her beautiful brown eyes.

"'I'm Lacy,' she said, suddenly looking bashful.

"'And where is your husband?'

"Luke interpreted for us, and it was then that her expression dramatically changed. I felt awkward and strange; I knew I had asked the wrong question. She suddenly turned away from us and began sobbing, unable to answer. My friend told her in French that it was all right, and she didn't have to answer. Whatever her story, I had a feeling that this would not be the last time we would face a situation like this. The farmer and his wife and now this young woman. It was all part of the fabric of horror and trauma that people here had suffered from the hands of their brutal captors.'

"'So, it's just you – taking care of the house and your daughter?' I asked, smiling at her baby.

"To that, she merely nodded.

"'I can't imagine what you've been through.'

"'No, you can't,' she said, turning around. 'my husband never saw his only daughter. I've been here, living alone ever since. One of my neighbors keeps an eye on me. She helped me with the birth. I don't know what I would have done without her. She, and my daughter here, are the jewels of my life.'

"'I understand,' I said, only beginning to comprehend the magnitude of the chaos wrought upon this land. I thought about the stories we were being told and then reflected on my life in London. I had been watching the German bombers coming in at night and killing thousands of my friends and neighbors. Every day on the news, we would hear about those who had been slaughtered the night before. I had even heard a rumor that our Prime Minister, Winston Churchill, would go up on the rooftop of 10 Downing Street and watch the German bombers come in.

He was never afraid and was one of the few who could keep strong the will of the English people against all odds. Yet, these were *personal* stories – these were stories about atrocities that had happened to *real* people, not just headlines in the news. And these stories would haunt them for the rest of their lives.

"'More tea?' she asked, smiling modestly and trying to be generous and thoughtful.

"My lieutenant shook his head. 'We really must be going,' he said, 'but if we may, can we refill our canteens from your well outside?'

"'But of course,' she said. 'I insist,' she added, smiling.

"We thanked her for her kindness and wished her and Emma well. She returned the gesture, giving each of us a hug and a peck on the cheek. Indeed, she was an extraordinary woman, having braved through what she had endured. At the same time, she had not been given the choice. Hers was about survival – not only for herself, but also her daughter.

"The rest of us left, but she grabbed the sleeve of Luke as we began walking off the porch. I looked back over my shoulder to see what was going on, and saw that she was talking and crying at the same time. Luke only stood there beside her listening and trying to be empathetic, as I knew he was. After several minutes, she gave him a peck on the cheek before he left to rejoin us. The look on his face was one of angst. He was clearly troubled by what he had heard."

Glen surprisingly stopped even as we waited for him to finish his part of the story. However, he only smiled back at us, looking around to see if his tale passed the test. When he saw people staring back at him, anticipating more, he merely shrugged and said, "That's it. That's all I have. Was it no good?"

"Marvelous," said Manny, reassuring him. "It really was quite something, and you left a perfect cliffhanger for the next person to pickup. Now, who's next? Does Glen need to pick someone or will someone finally volunteer?"

"I'll go," said a voice from the other side of the bus.

It was a small woman, sitting next to a man of about the same age. Both in their fifties, she wore a tan scarf with a black and burgundy checkered pattern in it. Fitting snugly around her head, it looked as though she were expecting a blizzard outside. As a result, her face looked squished together – flattened by the pressure of the wrap. Poking out in front, under the wrap, were strands of black and gray bangs that came down over her eyebrows but not far enough to impede her gaze.

As for her overcoat, she wore a heavy, wool knee-length Samet, probably once her mother's due to the style and age. It was a deep fuchsia with strands of olive and yellow here and there.

"And what is your name?" asked Manny.

"I'm Jamie. I'm his wife," she said, pointing to the man next to her. He lowered his head slightly but seemed used to her outspoken ways.

"I take it you two have been married for some time?" asked Manny.

"We're celebrating our thirtieth anniversary, and we're heading to Plymouth along the coast. We're just making a stop in Waterbury first."

"Wonderful," said Manny, smiling. "Congratulations. That's a real milestone - thirty years."

"Yes, I still put up with him after all these years," she said, jokingly.

He reached up and squeezed her hand lovingly. "I love you too," he said, grinning.

"So, why don't you see what you come up with," said Manny, extending the hat.

Jamie opened the paper and read the result: "I've got ... " she stopped and tried adjusting her glasses, but couldn't read it. She handed the paper to her husband who read it for her.

"Her paper reads: *Peace, Bible, faith*."

"Oh, I really like that," said Manny, grinning. "You should be inspired by something like that, don't you think?"

Jamie frowned. "I'm not sure," she admitted. "My faith hasn't been very strong lately. There's been so much tragedy in England with terrorism and all. How can anyone keep their faith through things like that?"

"That's for each person to figure out, I guess," Manny said. "We each have our own journey, don't we? We each have our own story to tell. And in our story, our young soldier has his too, doesn't he?"

"Yes, I guess you're right," said Jamie. "Things were hard back then. We tend to forget that. I guess it's all in your perspective of things, isn't it?"

"Jamie, the floor is yours," said Manny.

"Okay, well," she began, "the platoon was shaken by the stories told by the people they met. And as they were getting water from the well, the lieutenant looked back at the house and noticed the woman watching them from the window, pulling back the curtain and rocking her baby in her arms.

"'What did she say to you in the kitchen?' the lieutenant asked Luke, as we stood at the well.

"'She just talked about what things have been like since the Germans came to town,' Luke answered.

"'Did she say what happened to her husband?'

"'Yeah," said Luke, but stopping short of an explanation.

"'Well, what happened?' said Lt. Jack.

"'He's dead,' Luke responded, looking down. 'He was killed by the Germans shortly after they invaded France. They didn't come up here right away, but after they took Paris, they took the town up here. She said that lined up all the men on the outskirts of town. There the Germans had dug a long ditch. They asked them if they would voluntarly join the Nazi army. They shot every man who refused. She said that her husband was French and that he would always be French. He was also stubborn. There was nothing the Nazi's could do to change his mind. She said hundreds died that day.

"Lt. Jack looked back at the house, but the young woman and baby had gone. Only an empty window remained.

"Our platoon finished getting its water and began hiking on toward the next town. By now it was less than a kilometer away, and when we arrived we found two narrow streets lined with shops but abandoned and quiet. None of us liked the feeling there. It made our skin crawl. It was as if something were there, lurking, hiding, waiting for us.

"Cautiously, we approached, moving quickly to points of shelter. We knew the town should have been occupied by Germans, but it was strangely silent - vacant.

So, we moved slowly. Meter by meter we crept farther into town, our eyes darting left, right, up and down. I could feel my heart thumping in my chest, racing like a galloping horse. Something told me that at any time I might feel the searing pain of a piece of lead entering my skull. Cautiously, we moved forward ... then, it all let loose."

*****

CH 7 Ouistreham & Caen

But Jamie stopped and looked down at her husband.

"Sam, you're better at battles than I am. I'll let you take it from here."

Sam looked surprised but not shocked, as if this weren't the first time she had done this to him. I could only imagine the couple at a cocktail party telling another couple some story where she would do the same thing.

"Sure," he said, grudgingly, but standing up anyway. "Well, the rounds from a German MG42 machinegun began ripping off the side of the building where I was standing, and I ducked inside a doorway. Gunfire seemed to be coming from everywhere, but most likely there was only one nest someplace in that small town. If we were to retake it, we'd have to find that nest and destroy it.

"Jack, our lieutenant, motioned for us to split up - one group would stay put and continue to draw their fire, while the other two groups would flank left and right, hopefully able to spot the muzzle fire of the nest. We could tell the general direction of the rounds but couldn't spot exactly which building held the nest.

"I followed behind Rex, my sergeant, who took our group down a street with a series of small shops – all closed. We understood that peace and normalcy wouldn't return to this quaint town until the Nazi's were thrown out. But it would take a lot of blood and will to make that happen.

"Running quickly behind the sergeant, we could hear the clatter of a machine gun not far away. It was shooting straight down the main street at our main platoon body we left behind, but it wouldn't be easy for us, either. The nest would be well-guarded from below, so we would have to coordinate our attack with the other flank.

"Finally, there was another burst of fire, and this time I could see the muzzle flares. 'Up there,' I said to the sergeant, pointing toward the church bell tower. There were two machine guns up there -- the highest point in the town and the one most strategic in viewing nearly all angles of the streets below. We moved quickly to a narrow strand where shop awnings obscured the view."

"'We're covered here,' the sergeant said to us, seeing that the overhangs obscured the tower's view of us."

51

"'Yeah, but what about our guys on the other side? Our other flank?' I answered him."

"Our sergeant grabbed his football-sized walkie-talkie and pushed the *Talk* button. 'Victor, you need to pull your men back. They can see you coming from the church tower,' he warned.

"'Roger, that,' said Victor, but at that exact time, we heard a ferocious and long blast of automatic weapons coming from the tower and then return fire from across the street."

"*Tttttt … Tttttt …*" stuttered Sam, making the sound of machine gun fire.

"'Victor? Where are you?' asked our sergeant, again talking into the walkie-talkie. But he got no answer.

"'We'll draw their fire.' We heard the walkie-talkie squeak-out the voice of our lieutenant from the main company who was coming down the middle of the town street. 'Sergeant, you've got to take the church. You've got ten minutes. We can hold them off at least that long.'

"All hell broke loose from the lieutenant's men who fired from the protective cover of the shops along the main street up at the nest. The Germans concentrated their forces on the central threat while our squad ran under cover of the shop alleys on the left side of town to the base of the church. Our sergeant took the lead, but we were right behind him.

"Up against the massive, bullet-ridden front door of the church, we waited for the sergeant to give us the sign to make the next move. He raised his fist in the air with three things and in synch with the seconds, lowered each one until only a fist remained.

"Taking the butt of his rifle, Rex slammed it against the lock, springing the door. We burst through the opening, our guns pointed ahead and our trigger fingers twitching to pull back on the firing mechanism. It was then that all hell broke loose.

"I ran into the church and kept popping off shots as Nazi's jumped out to fire on us. Never being one of faith, I still felt strange shooting up the inside of a church. Yet, it had been the Germans, not us, who had defiled its sanctity.

"Against untold numbers of Nazi's the five of us stormed into the nave. Bullets whizzed past us like it was raining sideways. A buddy was shot through the chest as he scrambled around a pew to move closer toward the tower stairs. He lay motionless, his lifeless body draped over one of the pews. I took a bullet in the shoulder. It stung, but it wasn't serious.

"Once we took out the German soldiers in the nave, we fought toward the stairwell of the tower which would lead upstairs to the machinegun nest. Rex went first, keeping his back close to the inner wall of the stone stairs. I was right behind him, slinging my rifle across my back and pulling out my pistol. I raised it, ready to shoot anyone who showed his head from above in the tower.

"Shots rang down on us, but we kept firing, moving up a few stairs at a time. When we got close to the top, my sergeant stopped. This would be it. This would be the time we would either kill or be killed.

"I watched Rex look at me and take a deep breath. 'Cover me,' he said. I reloaded and began firing as fast as I could as he stormed the upper level. He ripped a hand grenade from his vest and pulled the pin just below upper hatch. However, a German pointed his Luger down at him and shot him through the forehead before he could release it. His body fell backwards on top of me, his hand releasing the detonation lever on the grenade.

"'*Shit!*' I cried. Rolling over, I grabbed the grenade out of his hand and threw it up through the hatch. Instantly, it exploded sending smoke and debris raining down on us. The smoke was so thick, we couldn't see a foot in front of us, so I kept firing my pistol as I continued climbing toward the top deck platform.

"Reaching the top, I could barely see anything but continued firing into the swirling sea of smoke and fumes. Soon, the wind had carried off the haze from the exploding grenade. In front of me lay four dead Germans slumped over the two machinegun stands they had used so effectively against us. Next to one of the bodies was a tattered, black Bible with three bullet holes in it, but none of the bullets had gone all the way through.

"*Why?* I thought. *Why couldn't it have saved Rex instead?*"

The shopkeeper finished, and we all fell silent. The story had been moving, and he had told it in such detail and with such emotion that we were left speechless.

"Another amazing story," said Manny. "Are you sure you weren't in the war?" he asked the man.

"No, but my grandfather was. He used to tell us stories like that all the time. That one really happened, but it was in a town in Germany, not in France."

Jamie beamed, and then chimed in. "Now that my husband is committed, it's his turn to pick a shard."

"What?" he answered, looking bewildered at being asked to go again. "But I just ..."

"Come on Sam. You're good at this. They want to hear more from you, don't you?" Jamie asked turning the rest of the bus.

"We want Sam! We want Sam!" the bus audience began to chant.

Sam blushed, and then raised his hand. "Okay, okay. Give me the hat," he said.

Sam pulled a scrap from the hat and read it aloud. "*Honesty, history and love.*" He looked upwards as if wanting guidance from the divine, but then lowered his chin and began again.

"What little faith I had I thought had been shaken by that event," he continued, "but in reality, it had made it stronger. Things that happen, happen for a reason they always said, and if you know your history, you can avoid the mistakes of the past and plan better for the future. I just wished that had happened in our case.

"We left Ouistreham after telling our command back in Noland T.dy about our progress. Unfortunately, we also had to relay the message that we had lost seven men in the process of retaking the town. That queer feeling I had when we had walked into that town had been borne out. I would never forget that sensation, and it wouldn't be long before I would feel it again.

"Our next stop was Caen. It was farther from the coast of England and so was less fortified by the Germans. Calais was farther east down the coast and was the place Hitler thought the Allies would land coming from England. It was heavily fortified, and it would be our next stop after Caen. Yet, that battle wouldn't come for another several days.

"Only six kilometers from Caen, we were to converge with another company of Allied troops who were also pushing east. Together, it was thought, we would be able to take Caen with relative ease before moving on to Calais. But that wouldn't be the case."

Unfortunately, my enthusiasm for history got in the way, and I interrupted the storekeeper. "But the Allies didn't take Caen until months later - around August. The Germans pushed several panzer – tank -- divisions into it to defend the city."

"Yes," said the shopkeeper, nodding in agreement. "But since this is *my* story, I'm going to move up the timeline a bit, if you don't mind?"

"Sorry. Yes, of course," I acknowledged, sheepishly. "Please ..."

"Thank you," said the shopkeeper, not angry, but just rather annoyed at me.

"So, it was some time later that we pressed into Caen. The Americans had succeeded in their operation against Cherbourg to the south -- I believe it was called Operation Cobra -- which redirected the panzer tanks and let us punch through, across the river, into Caen.

"Very good," I said, before being stared down by the rest of the bus. "Fine, I'll be quiet. I promise this time."

Sam cleared his voice once more. "Soooo, we fought our way into Caen under Operation Charnwood. We had over one hundred men in our company, and were up against over a thousand Nazis. They pulled a lot of their Panzer IV tanks out to defend Cherbourg, but there were still more than a dozen firing at us from the middle of the streets. Snipers in the buildings picked-off our men at an alarming rate, and we finally had to call in the airmen and their Hurricane bombers.

"I was with my lieutenant, Jack; my friend the interpreter, Luke; along with Marvin, Percy, Collin and William – oh, and I almost forgot Jason, our radio operator. These were guys from our original platoon that had stayed together as we crouched inside one of the abandoned buildings in the large town of Caen. We hunkered down, waiting for the skies to deliver a knockout punch.

"'So, you never told us about Rex,' said Luke, sitting next to me. 'I mean, you said he was killed, but you never said what happened.'

"I pulled out a pack of Marlboro's and tapped it against my palm to ease out one of the sticks. I lit it and sucked in the smoky vapor before answering, blowing out a gray cloud as I did.

"'He never felt nothin',' I answered, looking away and out the open front door. 'It was quick-like. There was no pain. It happened so fast, he didn't know what happened.'

"'Yeah,' said Luke, wanting to believe me. 'I figured as much. Sorry, bastard, he was. We'll miss 'im.'

"That was all that was said. It was all that needed to be said.

"Soon, we heard the low hum of engines. Craning our necks, we waited and watched, hoping to see our steel warriors in the sky, emblazoned with the British red and blue circle on the wings. Thank God, we weren't disappointed. Seconds later, the low hum had turned into a roar as two Hurricanes dropped out of the sky and let loose with their bombs.

Booom, booom … booom

"After the bombs hit their marks, another pair of bombers appeared. Wave after wave came and left, unloading their deadly cargos.

"But all those bombs didn't eliminate our problems – they only softened them up. It was then that we had to go door to door and flush out the Germans from their hiding places.

"The first building we entered was just across the bridge. It was four stories high with an equal number of gabled windows across the top. The windows were bordered by thin, caramel-brown shutters and white crisscrosses of panes that split each into eight squares. The building itself was an eggnog-flavor of stucco with dark chocolate beams running throughout it.

"My lieutenant rushed to the front of the building and waited for the rest of us to arrive before kicking in the door. We cleared the first floor before moving swiftly, silently to the second, then the third.

"It was the fourth floor where I again, felt a cold draft where there was no wind. We split-up, taking different sections of the floor. Lance corporal Percy and I took the back part of the floor, pointing our Enson into each room that was open and carefully releasing the latch on closed doors so we didn't telegraph our arrival.

"After clearing the third room, which was full of broken furniture, books scattered across the floor, and glass shards everywhere, we heard it.

Ttttttt!

Bang … bang, bang, bang!

Tttttttt … Ttttttt!

Bang … bang, bang!

"Percy and I rushed to where we heard the sounds – in the front of the building. Several bullets shredded the plaster wall just above my head. I dropped the floor, cradling my rifle and readjusting my helmet.

"'Percy, stay low,' I said, knowing he had been right behind me as we'd hurried to the scene of the fight. 'Percy?' I asked again, when I didn't hear any sound.

"I looked back. Percy lay with his head down."

"'Percy! We gotta go! Come on!'

"But Percy didn't move. I poked him, but he still didn't budge."

"Then, again, another blast of machine gun fire came from just down the hall, aimed in a different direction. This time the fire was returned by single shots from other Enson rifles that were positioned down a parallel hallway.

"I looked at my friend lying on the floor behind me. He was dead. The blood was spreading across the floor like a crimson lake overflowing its borders. I had the urge to jump out and just start shooting, firing at anything and everything in a mad fit of rage and revenge. But I didn't. We had trained for this stuff, and the one thing that had been drilled into my head was just that … *think first!*

"My comrades down the other hall continued to fire, and when I heard the German's stop to reload their guns, I rushed their spot. It was then I saw Marvin, Collin and Jason doing the same thing. Together, we emptied our magazines on the five Nazi's inside, making sure they wouldn't hurt any more of our boys.

"After savage fighting, we finally took the city. Unfortunately, I lost two more friends – Collin and William – before it was all over. Much of the city was destroyed from bombing. It took weeks to clear all the neighborhoods of Germans and German sympathizers. But eventually, we were able to liberate them.

"It was there that a few of us were taken in by a grateful soul, a shopkeeper, whose family and business had been destroyed by war. We talked one night, having a glass of Burgundy from a cellar we had uncovered during our house-to-house searches. I went out and brought back the case of six bottles, and all six were gone before the night was over. The shopkeeper, Maurice, and his wife, Lacina, had had two children, a son and daughter.

"The son had been taken by the Nazi's for the army, while the daughter had remained behind. Maurice believed his son had been killed in battle but was given no information. They had not heard from him in months. Their daughter, only eighteen, was shy and saddened by all that was happening around her.

"Her name was Melina, and she was beautiful. Young and with so much potential, she was timid and cautious about talking freely. She had suffered under the German's for the previous four years and had spent her teenage years in constant fear. She wasn't used to speaking up and sat in silence during our dinner. After she and her mother cleaned up the dishes, I asked the family to sit with us so we could talk.

"'How hard has it been for you?' I asked Melina who sat next to her mother.

"'Terrible,' she answered, in English. She had taken English in high school against her parent's wishes, but now it was coming in handy."

"'Why?' I asked.

"Melina glanced over at her father, and began to cry. 'It's all right,' her father told her in what French I could understand.

"It was then that Jason interrupted. I could tell he had taken a fancy to Melina and was trying to make her feel better.

"'I know it's hard,' Jason said sympathetically as I recall. 'When I was only eight, my Aunt Bridget came to the house unexpectedly. I remember answering the door and noticing her expression, which changed instantly from profound sadness to mere melancholy.

"'Oh, Jason, dear,' she said. 'I need to speak to your mother. Is she home?'

"'I ran and got mum, but when they went into the small front room to talk, I stayed just down the hall, listening in. I know I shouldn't have, but something had happened, and I was curious.'

"So, what did your aunt say?" I asked, as curious as Jason in our story.

The shopkeeper continued. "Well, Jason listened, and his aunt talked. But as the story unfolded between sobs he couldn't believe what he was hearing."

"'It can't be,' said Jason's mum. 'I just can't believe that. Please tell me it isn't so?'

"'No, Amanda, it's true. Our father has been arrested in a brothel.' Jason stopped for a moment to collect himself. 'It's just going to ruin our family. It's unforgivable, really. Pops? I ... I just can't come to grips with it, Audrey. Our own father!'

"Jason said his Aunt Bridget then let out a wail that shook the house. He slowly backed down the hallway, quiet-like, not wanting to make any noise or even breathe. It was only later when he found out that it was all true. His grandfather had been caught as a john, engaged in sex with a prostitute in downtown London. The family had been destroyed by it, as his mum's mother immediately kicked him out of the house and filed for divorce. Things had not been the same in Jason's own house since. His mum had felt betrayed by the father she had always loved and admired. He was her model of perfection, and it had been shattered.

"'Then, I got called up to serve in the British army,' said Jason, dryly. 'I left mum that cold, rainy day. I remember it like it was yesterday. She wept, and I wept. And together, we cried out our pain.'

"Then, Jason turned to Melina. 'So, I think I know what pain is,' he said. 'I think I've felt it too.'

"But Melina shook her head. 'No, I don't think you do,' she answered him. She lowered her gaze and again stared at the floor. Then, finally, she looked up. 'I haven't told you, father, but ...'

"'But what?' asked the shopkeeper.

"Melina looked down at her feet. She was still scared; still afraid of what might happen to her if she told someone the truth. 'They ... they raped me, father.'

"'Who? Who did this?' shouted her father, now standing up, his face red with rage. Who would do this to my little girl?"

"'The Germans. The soldiers. They ... they took turns with me after they took Caen. They took turns with me. It was awful - horrible. I will never be worthy of anyone again,' she said, sinking her face into her father's soiled shirt.

"I felt bad for her, and I looked upon that beautiful face with pity and sadness. I wanted to put my arms around her and love her so she could again feel wanted - - respected by her community. But they had stripped that away from her, depriving her of self-worth and self-respect. Whether she would ever have that again, no one could say.

"It was late, and we left their humble house. I thanked the shopkeeper and his wife for inviting us in, and I thanked his daughter Melina for her honesty. I knew it must have been hard for her to admit to what had happened. That would be a scar that would be forever healing.

"We were ordered to leave Caen immediately, as we had to push on. It seemed like we had been gone from home for years, but in fact, it had only been a few weeks. The war was still going on around us, and we had farther to go and much more to do before the nightmare would finally come to an end."

The shopkeeper smiled. He knew he had told another great tale, and we all agreed.

"Well, I need someone to follow that, but I realize it may be hard. Who feels up to the task?" asked Manny, looking around the bus.

With no takers, he glanced back at the shopkeeper. "Again, I'll have to rely on the last storyteller. You'll have to pick someone, mate," he said.

The shopkeeper looked around the bus, and his eyes settled on the next victim. "I think she looks like someone who can carry the torch for us," he said, pointing.

*****

CH 8 The Lecture

Before the next person could speak, our scene was interrupted when the doctor rushed back on board. Her face was riddled with concern, and she expressed urgency in her voice.

"We really need to get the coach driver to the hospital. I'm not sure how long he's going to last, His blood pressure is falling, and his breathing is getting shallow," she whispered to Manny, who was standing in the front.

Manny excused himself, leaving the bus with the doctor. He was gone for nearly a half hour, and those in the bus began to chatter. I finally got up and went out to check on them. When I stepped off the bus, I saw Manny bending over the driver with his hands on his chest and forehead. The doctor sat next to them, her hand on the driver's wrist measuring his pulse.

"How's he doing?" I asked, coming over to where they were huddled.

The doctor just shook her head. However, Manny didn't move. He knelt with his eyes closed as if deep in meditation. It struck me as odd, but then again, just about everything that evening had been strange.

I got back on the bus and took my seat, checking my watch and wondering when another car or lorry would cruise by to offer us help. Yet, instead, almost before I could get myself re-situated in my seat, Manny jumped back on the bus. He appeared jovial – almost cheerful.

"How is he?" I asked.

"He's fighting, but I think he'll make it. We just have to have faith," Manny said. "Now, where were we?"

"I think we were about ready to hear from this young lady, here," said Sam, the shopkeeper, smiling and again pointing.

It was the eldest woman on the bus. With a scarf wrapped about her head, she looked to be more than just a grandmother -- perhaps even a *great* grandmother. With her face wrapped tightly, the wrinkles around her eyes and neck seemed to be pulled taut to attempt a more-youthful image; however, there was no mistaking her age from dark circles and bags of sagging skin under her eyes, the ripples in her pursed lips, and the accordion folds prominent on both temples. She was no more than five feet tall, and her frail arms and hands stretched out as if she were accepting an Academy Award.

"Yes?" she answered, looking up at Manny.

Manny wasn't sure she understood him, so he asked her, "Ma'am, do you want to tell us a story? We've been talking about a platoon of British soldiers during World War II. You have a slip of paper that gives you three words to use in it. Can you continue the story and use those words? Do you think you can do that or would you like someone else to take your place?"

The old woman grinned faintly. Manny was unsure what she was trying to communicate, so he repeated himself. "I said, do you want to ..."

"I heard you plain enough," she answered bluntly, her head shaking slightly from tremors. "I've been listening to all of you and have enjoyed it very much. My father was in the war, you know. He landed on Sword Beach, so I know the story well, I'm afraid." She looked around, as if in search of a helpful face, and finally added, "I think I'd just like to give some insights to whomever you select next. I'm afraid my energy isn't what it used to be. But I have some stories to tell someone else who, perhaps, can share them with the rest of you and include the words I'm supposed to say."

"Very well," said Manny. "Then I will ask that young lady back there to come up and talk with you for a bit before she tells us your story. How would that be?"

The old lady smiled broadly. "That would be grand," she said, gesturing.

However, the young lady Manny had chosen was the sister of Theresa, and she didn't seem very happy about being chosen.

"I don't think so," said the young girl, shaking her head. "I'm not like my sister. I don't tell stories." She sat with her arms folded, unwilling to move.

The old woman pushed her feeble body up from her seat and came to the back of the bus to look at the girl with a scolding and disapproving face.

"Young woman," she began sternly, "I realize things have changed over the years since I was young. I understand the youth of today have different interests, activities and attitudes. However, if there is one thing that does not change, and that is manners. Treating one another with respect. Treating one's elders with respect. Treating others as you would like to be treated - *none* of that has changed, nor will it *ever* change. Those are truths whether you are ninety-nine or nineteen."

After this, the woman stood up a bit straighter.

"Tell me," she continued, "how does it harm you to come up here and listen to what I have to tell you? What harm will come to you if you tell us a story based on what I describe? Are you afraid you will be ridiculed? Are you afraid you will be treated poorly? If you are, then I ask you if any others here been so abused? I think not.

"I am older and have become wiser. I have learned through my life's experiences that no one is perfect. I have learned to enjoy the smallest bits of creativity and insight that come up all around us every second of our lives. Your life is short - whether you believe it or not. At your age, you don't believe that, but it's true. Like that, sitting here now, you can't see the empathetic and supportive group on this bus that is waiting for your story. Perhaps in your school, you see jealously, arrogance, spite, vengeance, deceit, and other evils -- these are all sins you would find from a parson's story. But you aren't going to get that attitude from anyone here. Not on this bus.

"Furthermore, when I was your age I listened to my elders. I respected what they had to say, even though I didn't always agree. Many of your generation have contempt for what my generation has built. You don't like the very principles and moralities that made Western civilization great. It's what my grandparents and my parents endured, sacrificed and died for that makes all this possible for you and your generation. The very story we are telling should have had some impact on you. From this story, you should see to what lengths our ancestors fought and died to win freedom from the tyranny and evils others can impose.

"Has my generation made mistakes? Sure. But name one that hasn't. We did our best, and in my opinion, we did a pretty damn good job.

"If you can't see all of this, then I feel sorry for you and for your generation. In fact, I'm glad I won't be around to see the future of our culture and civilization after your generation has led it slide off into a ditch."

The old woman lowered her head. She turned and began walking down the narrow aisle – back to her seat. She was half way to her seat when the young woman answered.

"Ma'am?" the young woman asked, "I'll sit with you, if it's still all right?"

The old woman got situated up front before she turned back to respond. "Well, of course I will. What are you waiting for?"

The young woman scampered to the front of the bus where she found an empty seat. Manny stood back in amazement and with satisfaction at what had just happened.

The young woman suddenly turned to him and asked, "I'm ready. Where's the hat?"

*****

CH 9 The Show Must Go On

Manny produced the hat, and the young woman reached in.

"By the way," said Manny, "what's your name? You're Theresa's sister, right?"

"Yeah, I'm Sandy," she said, pulling a piece of paper from the hat. She looked at it and read it straight away. "*Trees, wheels, and answers*."

"Good!" said the old lady. "I think we can find something in that."

"And what is your name?" asked Manny, leaning over toward the older woman.

"Oh, I'm Mildred. My father was in the great war, and many of the things you're talking about actually happened, sadly enough."

Sandy and Mildred talked for several minutes while Manny went outside to check on the driver. When he returned, he was frowning.

"What's wrong?" I asked, noticing his change.

"Dr. Morrison said the driver, Reed, was not doing well."

"Reed? Is that his name?" I asked.

Manny cocked his head. "Yes. You didn't know that?"

"No," I answered, embarrassed that I hadn't asked earlier. "But, how did you know?"

Manny shrugged. "I guess the doctor must have asked him."

"Well," said the barrister interrupting, "I just wish someone else would drive by so *we* could get out of here."

Finally, Sandy stood to address the bus. She was nervous, but seemed reconciled with her obligation to carry the torch and continue the saga.

"So, the story ended when the soldiers were leaving the town - Caen, right?" said Sandy. Behind her, Mildred was nodding approvingly.

"The road ahead was dusty," Sandy continued, "and littered with pieces of tanks and lorries that had been blown up by the Allies. The good guys had dropped bombs on them as they moved in a convoy toward Noland T.dy to try to stop the invasion.

"The wreckage on the road was bad, but the destruction off the roadside was worse. Whole areas were flattened by bombs and by tanks. Whole groves of trees were knocked down by the war. A lot of places that had been thick with trees now looked like plowed fields.

"Strangely, there was no one outside working or doing much of anything. It looked like everyone had disappeared - been beamed up to some spaceship or something. There were no farmers out, no shopkeepers out, no women out washing clothes or shopping at the stores. There were no cars on the road, or construction workers repairing the roadways. There were also no dogs or cats. The only things we saw were some cows and sheep.

"We figured the people were just afraid to come out of their homes - what with all the bombing and stuff going on. If they listened to their radios, they could tell it wasn't safe to be outside for *any* reason.

"But then we heard a loud noise coming down the road behind us. Usually, we'd jump into the bushes and hide, but this time we knew it was one of our own – a big convoy of jeeps, lorries and American tanks rolled up from behind us. The tanks, of course, had no wheels - only these things called tracks on the bottom. The tanks they called Cromwells for some reason. Anyway, they came up right behind us and the guys started talking to us right away. The Yanks were friendly too.

Sandy stopped and whispered, "Mildred wanted me to say that she saw some tanks one time in a museum. She said they were huge and awesome."

That made the rest of the bus laugh and Mildred beam.

"Anyway, we all felt stronger, knowing that we had that big *stuff* behind us. Our rifles were one thing, but those big tanks were something else.

"We moved to the side of the road to let the cranking of the tank treads roar by and a bunch of other. Falling in behind them, we could feel the heaviness of the load in our backpacks lighten just a bit. With our spirits lifted, we marched on with a little more spring in our step.

"That night, we played cards and invited some of the guys over from the tank group. Noland T. was the head tank guy ..."

"He's called the tank commander," I said in a whisper.

"Uh, yeah, the tank commander," said Sandy. "He was from Norwich - a nice enough guy. He was older than us - about twenty-eight, I'd guess -- and he told us he'd been fighting down in northern Africa, fighting the Germans down there. We had all kinds of questions for him -- about what it was like in Africa; about what the German soldiers were like; about battles he'd fought in -- all kinds of stuff.

"He told us it was like a desert down there -- hot and dry. The sand blew everywhere and got into everything. He said the tanks often didn't work right because they got jammed with sand – same with their rifles. They tried to put tarps over the equipment, but the sand still managed to get into things, he said.

"He also talked about the nasty sandstorms that would roll across the land. They were blinding, and most times the men could only see about a foot or two in front of their faces. He said, everything stopped then. They ended up wrapping their guns in sailcloth to keep as much sand from getting in them as they could. The lorries and even some tanks got stuck in the sand drifts.

"After that, most of us felt better about being stuck in northern France than in northern Africa. Sure, the winds off the English Channel could be cold, but it seemed far better than the super-hot days in the desert followed by freezing cold nights."

Sandy leaned over to the old woman and whispered something. Mildred answered, "No, no. You did a wonderful job. Wonderful!"

"I agree," said Manny, smiling and clapping for her. "So, who will be next?"

"Why don't you give it a go?" Mildred asked as she nudged the middle-aged man next to her.

"Me? No, I couldn't possibly ..." he answered.

"Come on," she prodded. "What's your name, anyway?"

"I'm Charlie," he said.

Charlie was tall – probably the tallest one on the coach. He was up in years, but not as old as Mildred. Probably in his early sixties, Charlie looked like he had struggled in life. His face was lightly pitted by the scars of youthful acne and the stresses of years gone by. With short, cropped black hair, his brow was wide and eyes deep set. There was still the flicker of energy burning within him, but even his soiled fingers and calloused hands suggested his struggles had been hard and long.

"So, Charlie, what is it that you do for a living?" she continued, doing Manny's job for him.

"I own a shop -- it's a machine shop in the heart of Manchester. Me and my family have worked it for years. My two boys are still in school, and they help now and again with some of the work. It puts food on the table for us."

"Why are you traveling to Waterbury, then?" asked Manny.

"Me brother lives there," said Charlie. "He's me older brother. I don't get to see him or his wife often. Me wife couldn't come with me since she's minding the business at home."

Manny extended his arm and held out the hat. "Here you go," he said, offering no alternative.

Charlie sighed and gave a slight shake of his head. He reached in and pulled out a paper. "*It says Coke, stamps, and balance*." He looked completely baffled. "I just don't know what to make of this," he said, just like some of the others. "I'm afraid I'm not going to be of much help."

"Well, then pick someone to help you," said Manny. "There are plenty of people here on the bus who would be more than happy to help."

Charlie looked around and found a friendly face not far away. "Can you help me?" he asked. It was Mildred, the old lady next to him.

"Sure," she said, smiling. "I'd be glad to."

If I hadn't known better, I would have said that she was relishing the time on the bus. The grin on her face showed me that she hadn't felt that way in a long, long time. Someone needed her, and she was grateful.

The two talked for quite a while before Charlie felt ready, and he stood in front of the group - nervous but determined.

"Okay, then," he started, "I've got *Coke*, *balance*, and *stamps*, right?" He cleared his throat. "So, our tank commander friend looked around carefully, and seeing that no one else was looking, he pulled out a silver flask with his initials engraved on it: **WRG**. I said to him, 'what's the R stand for?' as we already knew his name was Will Grantham.

"'Oh, that's me mum's maiden name: Riley. She's Irish, ya' see,' he said. Then he took a swig of whatever he had in that flask and began passing it around.

"When it came to me, I took a sniff. It was strong, and I wasn't so sure what it was. But he laughed at me, like I was some prissy pawn and said, 'Too strong for ya', lad?'

"'course not,' I answered taking a quick nip. It burned the back of me throat like someone had shoved a red-hot poker into me mouth. Then, I could feel it searing my gullet all the way down. *'Goot*,' I squeaked at him with a high-pitched voice. Again, he laughed.

"'So, how long you boys been out here?' Will asked. His face was intense, but he seemed genuinely interested in everyone and everything. Even though he was a little older than us, he seemed a *lot* older. He had seen death up close, and it hadn't bother him much – not like it did most of us. He told his stories like he was telling us about going to the corner shop for some smokes. Most of his stories were dark and told of the brutality of the Germans. Still, we didn't feel like he was telling us just to shock us. He wasn't that kind of guy. He was just ... well ... who he was; take him or leave him.

"Will had dark, wavy hair and thick, matching eyebrows. I felt like his family was dirt poor – that he didn't know what money really meant. He had probably enlisted just to get a job and make some money, but then he'd gotten caught up in the patriotism thing. He had a good heart – that he did.

"He was someone who was used to doing what he wanted, when he wanted. Yet, the British army had changed all of that. He had probably matured a lot in the two years he'd been fighting for the homeland. He was proud to be a British soldier now – proud of his country, his people, the cause. He had found something that was bigger than himself, and he was wearing it well.

"'So, what are your hobbies back home?' someone asked him.

"'Hobbies?' he said, somewhat surprised. 'Well, me pops was a stamp collector. That's something he did as long as I can remember. He'd sit me down at the kitchen table with the red checkered table cloth spread across it, and he'd pull out his prized stamps. Lifting them up with his tweezers, he would get out his little, black eyepiece to examine them -- one-by-one. Then, he'd hand the tweezers to me for me to look. I'd glance through the glass piece, but it would just look like some stupid stamp to me. I guess I never appreciated what it was that he saw in it. But somehow, now I think I do.'

"'You appreciate stamp collecting?' asked someone else.

"'No, I appreciate the fact that pops liked it. It was something that made *him* happy. It didn't matter if it made *me* happy, and I didn't get that then. He wanted to share something that made *him* happy. I didn't get that. I thought he was just being selfish, you know. But the more I've thought about it, the more I think I understand. Sure, it would have been great if I had been interested, but all he was trying to do was bond with me. He wanted – no – he needed that connection to me.'

"Will put his head down and then added, 'I feel bad now because I told him I thought stamps were dumb and that I didn't know why he wasted his time on them. My dad had looked sad at first, and I thought it was because I said nasty things about his hobby. Now, I get that he was sad about the fact we couldn't bond over something like that."

"Shrugging his shoulders, Will acted like it didn't bother him, but then he said, 'My dad died three weeks later, after I'd already deployed. I couldn't go home for the funeral, so I never saw his face again.'

Charlie choked up a bit, as if this story were more personal than he was letting on.

"'Later, pops would get two colas out of the frig and pop one for each of us. It was a special time for us. We would sit there, and I would just watch him. It felt good, even though I guess I was just a little bored. I didn't get to spend a lot of time with my father. He was always so busy at the steel yards.'

"You miss him," I said, seeing the sorrow in his face.

"Yeah, I miss him a lot. Pops died last year. They said he had cancer. I was in Australia when he passed, and I couldn't get home. Mum sent me the note. I felt alone and helpless half way around the world. There was nothing I could do for me mum or for me pops. It's a feeling I never want to have again."

I watched as this brave, hearty man wiped the tears away from his eyes. It hurt him to talk about it, and he took a couple deep sighs.

"Anyway," Charlie said, trying to continue his story. "So, Will took a swig from his flask before sending it around the circle again.

"'It's all just part of life, ain't it?' Will said. 'They call it the Circle of Life, I think. You have kids so they can carry the torch for you after you die, right? Any of you have kids?'

"The rest of us in the group shook our heads."

"'No,' said Luke. 'Hell, we're not even married. Some of us don't even have girl friends back home.'

"'A shame,' said Will. 'It would suck to die without having any kid to follow in your footsteps, I think. I dunno. This war does funny things to your head, ya' know."

"His words hit me hard. I hadn't thought that much about it, but he was right. If I died, there'd be no one after me. Then, what would the purpose of my life be? Maybe to win a war and save the world? Maybe. And maybe that would be okay. I really wasn't sure."

"'So,' Will continued, 'when I get home, I'm gonna get married to my girl and have kids.' He took a big swig from his flask as it came his way again. He wiped his mouth on his sleeve before sending it on around the circle.

"'So, you gotta sweetheart at home then?' Percy asked him.

"'I did, but I haven't heard from her in a while. I'm afraid someone else got to her. There's not much you can do about that when you're a thousand miles away. I may have to find me another girl when I get home. That'll be hard, but, hey, that's life, right?'

"'You love her -- your girl, that is?' asked Max, another private in our group.

Charlie sighed again. "Now, what didn't I cover?" he asked, looking around the bus.

"You didn't cover *balance*," said the attorney on the bus, surprisingly listening to what he had said.

"Oh, I thought it was *circle*, for some reason," he said, shaking his head. "Okay, well, so Will finished his story, and by that time we was pretty drunk -- me especially, since I wasn't used to anything stronger than beer. I turned in and quick fell asleep. But I wasn't woke-up by revelry. Instead, I heard artillery shells going off nearby. They were ours, and they were shooting at something overhead. When I looked up into the dark sky, I could tell what it was. The German Luftwaffe was flying overhead on their way to London. They were going to bomb the city. We all knew what that meant – previous runs had killed thousands, and we knew this one would do the same. I'd got letters from Mum about the bombs that fell on London earlier in the war, but she didn't say anything about them now. I just figured that they had stopped. But it was clear that they hadn't. By the look of things, there were about fifty bombers flying over us, and our artillery was doing its damnedest to stop them.

"I rolled over and saw my lieutenant was looking at the same thing. 'I thought our invasion had stopped their bombing of London,' I said to Jack, who looked as worried as I did.

"'Guess not,' Jack answered. 'I guess the balance of power hasn't changed yet. We're still on defense. It looks like we still have a ways to go.'

"And indeed we did. The war was far from over. We would learn that painfully during the following days."

Charlie finished and sat down, proud of himself. I was quite impressed with his narration and felt myself anxious, anticipating who would be next and where they would take us.

*****

CH 10 So Close

"I think we're on a roll," said Manny, clearly pleased with what he'd heard. "If I were you, I would step up now. The story is getting so good it's becoming harder and harder to tell the next tale. So, who wants to be next?"

It was no longer a matter of prodding someone to reach into the hat. Now, it was about selecting who would be next.

"Okay, you there, what's your name?" asked Manny.

"I'm Eugene. I'm an engineer who's been working in one of the weapons factories in Birmingham. I got a few days off, and I'm visiting family in Manchester and in Waterbury. Since the threat of war in the Middle East has increased, my factory has been busy. I don't get to take much time, so it's going to be a quick trip."

"What are you working on?" asked Manny, "I mean, what project are you working on?"

Eugene shook his head. "I'm afraid Mr. Churchill wouldn't be very happy with me if I told you," he said laughing, "however, I *can* tell you it's good stuff."

"Well, it's good to know that Mr. Churchill can rest easily in his grave knowing that we have such outstanding people working in our defense industry. So, Eugene, please pick a slip."

Eugene pulled out a folded sheet and read the results. "*Image*, *Frame* and *Cars*," he said. Then, he added, "I can do this on my own."

He only thought about things for a few moments before he cleared his throat and began.

"So, the Allied guns were blazing, sending shells high into the air. We saw that they weren't hitting a lot, but once in a while they did hit a bomber, and it would burst into flames. We would cheer as the plane smoked and crashed into the English Channel in the distance.

"I wondered where our Spitfires were, but it seemed they hadn't yet spotted the enemy flying toward their homeland. It was discouraging, but at least the big guns they'd brought over on freighters were doing some damage.

"When dawn finally came, the skies were clear and blue again, as if God had taken a giant eraser and blotted out all the dark smoke and nastiness of the German planes from the sky. The shells we used were the 3.7 inch variety, but most of them missed their mark. The QF AA guns were effective, but back in the day, they weren't guided by lasers like they are now to make them accurate.

"Still, even an hour after sunrise, my ears were still ringing from the artillery shelling. We never heard how many of the Luftwaffe were shot down, but it sounded like even though many were obliterated before reaching London, many others still got through. Those caused heavy casualties in the city – killing hundreds every time they bombed.

"After breakfast, we headed out. The Willies or jeeps used by the upper officers were outnumbered by the lorries trucking in supplies for us. And in one of the Willies was a photographer - someone from *Life Magazine*, I believe. He was assigned to get pictures of things for his magazine.

"I remember that his name was Frank -- a short, small-bodied gent, probably no more than five feet at the most. He was American, of course, and had a funny accent, like he came from New York -- maybe the Bronx or something. Anyway, he had a fancy camera. He called it a Kodak 35, and he said it took really good *pitchures*, as he called them. So, I asked him what sorts of *pitchures* he'd been taking.

"'All sorts of things,' he told me. 'I was there at D-day on Utah beach. Got some great *pitchures*, but it was a bloodbath - horrible. Our guys fought like hell though. It was tough getting everything into the frame - you know, the battle was so broad and wide. And the wind and sea spray clouded my lenses, making it hard to keep them clean. I'm sure I got water spots on some of them, but at least the water didn't destroy my camera like it did other photojournalists, I know.'

"Then I asked him if there was one image that came to his mind - one that he would never be able to get out of his head, and he said 'Yes. I took a picture of a marine on the beach. He was just lying there with his gun pointing up at the machine gun nests above him. I thought he was just waiting for that one shot, you know, that one kill shot. But he was there a long time. So, I crawled over to him. I asked him if he was okay, but he didn't answer me. He only kept looking up at the side of the cliff. Then, I put my hand on his shoulder and said, '"Hey, bud. It's okay, you know. Everything will be okay."' His body rolled over, and I could see that the other side of his face was completely gone. He was dead. That shook me, you know. That will always bother me as long as I live.'"

"We continued marching along the dirt road toward our new objective which we were told was Le Mans, about two hundred kilometers south from us. There weren't a lot of towns along the way, but there was one that had an old car the farmer was probably trying to rebuild. It was a Mercer Model C Speedster, probably originally built in 1910 or so. She needed a lot of work, but it wasn't something you saw very often over there. A bright yellow -- almost canary yellow color -- she stood out in the field like a glow-bug at midnight. It was hard to believe she hadn't taken any hits from bombs or machine guns, but there she was all the same. It made me think of my MG M-Type that I had at home. I'd been working on it for years, trying to get it back in running condition. A royal blue, that baby was my first love - well, at least after my girlfriend. I couldn't wait to get back to England and start working on her, but that would be a long time off."

Eugene smiled when he'd finished. "Was that okay?" he asked.

"Brilliant," said Manny.

It was then that we bus heard a noise outside coming down the road. Everyone got excited, and we looked out our blackened windows hoping the sound was from our rescue car. As the lights grew closer, we could tell it was coming at a high speed. A few at the front of the bus jumped off, staying alongside the roadway but waving their arms furiously to catch the driver's attention. I followed them, joining in the optimism.

But as we continued to wave and shout, we saw the driver was not slowing - not in the least. Instead, he was weaving, crossing the center line at various points and then steering the vehicle back onto the left side where he belonged. Whizzing by the coach, he gave us no heed, continuing down the road and disappearing as if he had never been there.

"What's wrong with people?" I said to some others around us.

It was Manny who came over to me. "Some people just don't care about others, unfortunately. But, you know that already. They go through life only caring about themselves and getting to their next stop. Their world is egocentric - the sun and planets revolve around them and their center of gravity. Perhaps when they get older they'll see that life is about more than that - it's about friends and family for sure, but it's about others too. It's also about their fellow man."

"And we could have been *their* friend, if they'd only stopped," I added.

"Yes," said Manny, smiling, "unless we give others the time of day, how can we know what time it is?"

We clamored back onto the coach and hoped we would hear that sound again soon from another car or lorry coming down the road. I could only think, no pray, that the next person would be far kinder.

As I got on the bus, I noticed that Manny didn't return with the rest of us; so, I went looking for him. The doctor was still sitting next to the coach driver, and I asked her if she had seen Manny.

"He told me he was going to go get us help," she answered me. "But before he left, he gave the driver a morsel of something and then a sip from his canteen."

"Which way did Manny go?" I asked, surprised he would leave without saying goodbye. "Did he walk up the road this way or that way?" I continued, pointing in both directions.

"Oh, he didn't walk up the road. He went back into the woods. I can't explain it. When I called to him to ask him about that, he only waved and smiled. Then, he just vanished."

"Odd," I said, shaking my head.

I started to go back to the coach when the doctor said to me, "Oh, he also said to give you this." She held out the hat he had been using for our storytelling. Inside were the rest of the folded pieces of paper.

I took the hat back inside the coach and stood in front of everyone, explaining what had happened. "So, I don't know if you want to continue the story or stop since Manny isn't here," I said, shrugging my shoulders with indifference.

"Let's keep going," said the old lady in front. "I'm really enjoying this!"

It seemed the rest of my coachmates felt the same. "Alright then, who wants to go next?"

*****

CH 11 Fort Falaise

"Why don't *you* go, Jansen?" Eugene asked the man sitting next to him.

"I wouldn't be any good at this," said the man, about the same age as his mate.

"Give it a try. I think you should. Just try," pleaded his friend.

"And what do you do, Jansen?" I asked.

"Oh, I'm an engineer like Eugene here," he said.

"No, you're not," countered Eugene. "He's a physicist - and a very good one too. He's just had a bit of a rough time lately, and this coach trip hasn't made it any easier."

Jansen smiled graciously, but then only held out his hand as if asking me to show him the hat, which I did. He reached in and pulled out a paper.

"*Cool, Jealousy, Lost. Wow*," he said, finishing the words. Then he corrected himself, "No, *wow* is not one of the words. I just added that inflection on my own."

It was then that I wished Manny had still been there. Obviously, there was someone on board who was hurting, but without him, I didn't know how to reach out to help.

"Let's start where we left off, before we get lost in all of this," said Jansen. "We had just finished with the cool MG car – one I've always been jealous of -- when Eugene finished his narration. Wow!" he added, laughing.

Everyone in the coach groaned.

"Should we let him get by with that?" I asked.

Although many in the coach shook their heads, I gave him my empathy and the benefit of the doubt. "We'll let it go this time, Jansen, but let's make your three-word story a little bit longer, all right?"

"Cool!" Jansen said again, joking. "But seriously, the road to Le Mans was more dangerous than we had anticipated. It was there we first discovered that the way was not clear - not so easily crossed.

"My part of the story will tell of Frank, our army photographer. He was sometimes off, wandering dangerously into the surroundings taking photos of different things other than combat. He enjoyed nature and would take pictures of birds and animals, especially when he found something striking or beautiful. He had a wonderful eye for things - a true artist. There weren't many like him, and that was probably why he was a photojournalist for a magazine as significant as *Life*. Back then, it was *the* magazine for photographers. Once you were there or at *National Geographic* you were set.

"Anyway, it was late one afternoon when I saw him out of the corner of my eye. He had left the main road and gone off into one of the fields. Not more than a few minutes later, we heard this explosion. It sounded like a bomb had been dropped nearby, and I guess in some ways it had. I rushed to where the spray of dirt was settling and saw Frank. I saw what I feared. He lay in the field, face-down. His big, black metal camera was more than fifteen meters away from his body. Like its owner, it lay in pieces – fragments scattered around and most lost forever.

"I could see immediately that Frank was missing pieces too. His left arm was blown off, and he was bleeding from his head. I rushed to him, and we quickly put a tourniquet on his arm before he bled-out. Lifting him up, he rushed him to one of the lorries who sped him back to the field hospital back in Caen.

"Watching the lorry belch blue smoke as it chugged away from the troops, I felt bad for him. He was just doing his job when he stepped on a mine. The Germans had laid mines all around the French countryside. We called them Bouncing Betty's or S mines because when they were triggered they would fly into the air before exploding overhead. Without an arm, it would certainly be hard for him to continue on for *Life* or for any other magazine. I could only hope he would find a way to adapt, as many who left the battlefield would have to do.

"Our lieutenant got out his map, and I asked him if we were lost. He said no, that he was just looking to see if there was another route to Le Mans - one that might not have any land mines. But after watching him, I could tell he wasn't so sure.

"Later that same day, when the cool breezes began blowing in off the Channel, we came to a small town called Cintheaux. It was there we started taking small arms fire. It wouldn't be long before we were embroiled in the firefight of our lives – the one we would later call, the Falaise Pocket."

Here Jansen stopped to take a breath. It was clear he knew more about what happened back then than he had let on. I sensed in him a kindred spirit - a love of history, as I did. And, I eagerly awaited the rest of his story.

"Go on, Jansen ..." I said.

"Those who didn't fight in Falaise would later be jealous of those who did. But jealousy comes sometimes only if you haven't personally experienced it. It's not like when you see someone with better clothes or a better life; you might wish you had that too. It's human nature. But when it's something bad, and you wish you had the same *bragging* rights as they say in America – well that's something different.

"I'd say it's an insecurity – that you only wish you could tell the same story to be someone important. But for those who lived through the nightmare, it isn't something to boast about, and most say nothing about it at all the rest of their lives. That's odd, wouldn't you say?

"Anyway, when it came to the Battle of Falaise Pocket, it was odd that men wished they had been there. Why? Most did not live to tell about it. It is by fate that *we* were put there at that day and time - to fight against the machines of death thrown at us by the Nazis.

"It was early August, and we were approaching Falaise. We knew the town was heavily fortified with German Panzer divisions - particularly those of Field Marshal von Kluge, but we were part of a grander strategy devised by Generals Eisenhower of America and Montgomery of Britain. We were supposed to surround the Germans in Falaise and cut them off from retreat to the east.

"Our attack started on the morning of the twelfth of August, and with air support above, we began pounding the German line. Bullets flew by my helmet as we made our way, yard by yard closer to the town square. The smoke and smell of burning tires in the town were overwhelming. To make visibility even worse, the skies were dark with artillery shell explosions and those from the German Panzer tanks raining down bits and pieces of buildings all around us. Then, every hour or so, we would get the hand signal from the lieutenant to advance. As the Germans pulled back, we pushed on.

"Advance!" came the signal from the lieutenant, gesturing with his hand.

"It was then that fate struck. Shells had been pummeling the ground all around us, but none had come too close. We were in a grove of trees just outside the high, fortified walls of the fort where the Germans were embedded. I remember the tall, round turret-like building that was the main structure; it was just above us.

"Just as we began our charge, two shells exploded. I can still hear the ringing in my ears to this day. The force threw many of us up into the air, and I landed at least five or six meters from where I'd been standing. It took me a few minutes to come around and when I opened my eyes, all I could see was thick, choking smoke. I started coughing and couldn't seem to stop. My eyes watered, and I could feel blood oozing into my uniform from my right shoulder. I reached for my sleeve and saw it was in tatters, a mix of red goo and cotton threads.

"Lieutenant?" I called out. "Luke? Marvin? Is anyone there?"

I fought through the curtain of blackness until I found spots where I could see again. "Bart? Are you there?"

Finally, I spotted my lieutenant who was crouched over the body of one of ours. "Lieutenant? Who ..."

"It's Bart and Tony ..." he began, putting his fingers on Bart's eyelids and pushing them shut.

Two friends - Bart from Derby and Tony from Chester, both died when a shell exploded not thirty feet from me. I was coming out from behind a tree at the time and was saved. They were not; they died instantly. *How strange that life can be so capricious?* I thought. *Why them and not me?* I would ask myself that question for the rest of my life.

"The fighting wasn't over in a day as per the grand plan. It took weeks before we were able to march uncontested into Falaise. By then, the remaining Germans were trapped and captured. However, many other Nazis had escaped east to fight another day."

"I hope that was okay. That's about all I can think of at the moment ... just tried to further the story a bit," Jansen said, sitting down in his coach seat.

"Nice," I commented. "I appreciate your history background. All very good and on point, I might say. So, we're still marching on, I guess. Who wants to carry the baton now?"

I glanced around the coach and saw many eager faces, but one struck me as appropriate at that juncture. It was a man with a collar. "Father?" I asked.

However, he corrected me. "No, I'm a minister. You can call me Patrick, and yes, I'd be glad to carry on the torch."

He reached into the hat and read his piece. "*Sweat, Labor, Moon*," he said, but then he corrected himself and said, "I think it's supposed to be *Sweet*," he said, trying to figure out the writing. "I'll go with sweet. It's a much nicer word."

So, Minister Patrick stood up and began to tell his story.

*****

CH 12 Minister Patrick

"I must say," began Minister Patrick, "I don't know as much about the war as others here, but I will do my best. Anyway, after the Battle of Falaise, we camped near a nunnery which also cared for the children at the orphanage. The orphanage had been part of the nunnery for hundreds of years, and unfortunately, they had never run out of a supply of new customers.

"It was Sister Margaret who greeted us at the door. At first, she was afraid to let us in, but when we carried food supplies and medicine for them, she smiled and eagerly showed us to the infirmary. There were many children there - most were malnourished, and some even had life-threatening diseases. After depositing our crates, sister took us around the room where they kept their young patients. It was stark with nothing more than steel-framed beds with straw mattresses and bent bedpans. The conditions were clean, but that was about the only care the nuns could give – that and as many prayers as they could muster.

"'And this is Mona,' said Sister Margaret, walking up to the small bed of a little girl. Mona peered out from her bed, her big, brown eyes fearful of the strangers who had stopped to see her. 'Mona is eleven. She was brought to us after her mother and father were killed when the invasion took place in 1940. She suffered a fracture to her skull, but she has mended nicely - at least her body has. She still suffers nightmares of that night when the Germans came to their home and shot her parents and her brother. They took her small body and threw her off a balcony, thinking they'd killed her. But she's our little survivor. That she is.'

"I smiled at Mona, whose mouth tried to lift its corners and smile back, but couldn't.

"'She's such a sweet child,' I said to the sister. 'It's so tragic that she had to suffer like this.'

"'And this is Claude,' said the nun, taking us to the bed next to Mona's. 'He has a nerve disease, but we aren't able to diagnose what it is. Perhaps now he can get the help he needs too.'

"We walked around to several other children's beds, each with their own malady. There was so much that needed to be done, and our medicines would only scratch the surface of what the nuns really needed. But at least it was something, and I was glad for that.

"It was then that I noticed there were no crucifixes on the walls. I asked Sister Margaret about that. 'All the walls are barren,' I said. 'Why is it that you have no crosses hanging up?'

"'Hitler doesn't believe in Christianity. He forbade us from putting them up,' she said. 'They say he is the devil himself. I don't know. I try to be pious and think the best of people; however, after what I've seen these past four years, I believe that there is a evil at the very least. Is Hitler a demon? I'll leave that for others to decide.'

"'You must love these kids very much,' I said to her, seeing the pain in the faces of the children and the same in Sister Margaret. 'You must struggle with not being able to do for them what you want … what they need … every day.'

"Sister smiled graciously. 'It's a struggle,' she answered, 'but it's also a labor of love. You must have faith. It sounds simplistic, but you must believe in God and His ability to give them comfort - if not here, then in Heaven. That's what keeps you going. That's what helps you get through a nightmare like this.'

"We walked out toward the open courtyard in the center of the nunnery. It was peaceful there.

"'Do you hear that?' she said to me as we stood without moving in the calm, cloudless night. The moon was full and bright overhead, offering soothing relief to a stormy time.

"'No,' I said, hearing nothing.

"She smiled. 'That's right. I don't hear anything either. Isn't it wonderful? It's peaceful. It's serene. It sounds like … well … it sounds like my old village.'

"'Where is that?' I asked.

"'Falaise. I was raised there. It was always peaceful there. It was always quiet. It was a slice of heaven. Perhaps, now it can be again.'

"My thoughts turned quickly to my fallen companions, Bart and Tony. 'It's nothing like that now,' I answered. 'We can only pray that it returns to the paradise you described.'

"She turned to me and took my hands. 'Thank you,' she said. 'Thank you for returning this small piece of heaven I thought we'd lost forever. Although I've never lost my faith, it was certainly tested. I'm glad I never gave it up. Deep down, I knew God wouldn't forsake us. He wouldn't abandon these poor children. They are His children after all.'

"'They *are* God's children,' I said to her. 'We have a responsibility to them and if not to them, then to whom?'

"'Bless you, my son,' she answered, giving me the sign of the cross.

"I left the nunnery feeling a sense of hope. I felt I had a purpose in life. The only thing I didn't know was whether my next thirty or sixty days would let me fulfill it."

Minister Patrick sat down. He had done well, and we all felt more hopeful after his story, if not a bit more spiritual.

"Thank you, Patrick," I said, continuing to lead the group. "We still have a few more pieces inside here. Who wants to speak next?"

It was a quiet man sitting across the coach who stood and pushed his black glasses back up on his nose. "I'm Niles, and I'm an accountant," he admitted. "This isn't something I normally do. But, well, heck -- why not?"

"So, what did you get?" I asked him as he unfolded the paper.

"I have *Apricots, Family, and Memories.*"

I winced. Of all the people to get a hard one, I felt sorry for him. "All right then, let's see what you have for us."

Without hesitating, Niles began with surprising aplomb.

"The road to Le Mans was less eventful from that point south. The Germans were in retreat, and there was less opposition as we ploughed on. At one point, when we stopped for a canteen break, I asked the lieutenant about his home town and family. He never talked much, especially to us enlisted men. Everyone just called him lieutenant, of course, but he did have a name: Jonathon – Jack -- Rowlins. In fact, he was a very interesting chap once you got to know him.

"So, while the rest of us talked and passed around our cigarettes, Lieutenant Jack would just get out a book and read. This time, he wasn't reading. Instead, he held his book in his lap, staring out across an open field.

"'So, lieutenant, sir,' I said, coming up to him, 'where are you from -- if you don't mind my asking?'

"'A town between Glasgow and Edinburgh, called Kirkcaldy,' he said with a bashful smile.

"'Oh, you're a Scott, then?' I said. 'But you don't sound Scottish?'

"He laughed, 'Yeah, I get that all the time. My parents are Brits, but they moved to Scotland after they were married. They bought a small farm up there after the Great War - number one - and wanted to settle down.'

"'Got any brothers or sisters, then?'

"'Two older sisters who keep things going at home. They're both married with kids all ready. It's just me now that lives with my parents.'

"I could tell he wasn't the kind of guy to talk on and on about his family, so I changed the subject. 'I noticed you've been reading your book a lot lately. What's it about?'

"The lieutenant picked his book up and looked at the cover. 'Oh, this? This is just about how to grow apricots.'

"'What? You're pulling me leg,' I answered.

"'No, really. I've always wanted a grove of apricot trees. This tells how to grow 'em, manage 'em, and all that.'

"'How do you grow apricot trees? Don't they grown in hot climates, like Italy? How are you going to grow them in Scotland?' I asked.

"'Oh, gosh no,' said the lieutenant. 'Apricots are hardier than peaches. You can grow apricots in cold weather - down to minus twenty Celsius. But they'll grow in Mediterranean climates as well. At least that's what my book tells me. You see there are many varieties of apricot trees, but there are also three main sizes - the standard, dwarf and mini's. I would plant the dwarfs because we don't have as much room on the farm as I would need for the bigger ones. They just take good, well-drained soil, and about eight-to-ten hours of sun per day. It's really not hard to grow them. You just need to watch out for the insects and diseases.'

"'I'm sure you'll know all about that by the time you finish your book on them,' I said.

"'I hope so,' said the lieutenant, picking up his book and opening it to where he left off.

"By that time, we were ordered again to head out. It was noon, and we still had a long march ahead of us. But before we began, the lieutenant put his hand on my shoulder and said, 'I didn't get to ask you about your home town, sergeant.'

"I smiled at him and answered, 'We can talk more at our next stop,' I said.

"It's funny though, I still remember that talk all these years later whenever I buy an apricot at the grocers. I guess those are the memories you just never let go of -- the things they say are sparked by smells and sounds. Even though I wasn't smelling those apricots while we were sitting there, they were so vivid in my mind, I could almost taste them. To this day, I love the smell and taste of an apricot. And, I guess I can thank Lieutenant Mike for that."

It was a quick story, but with what he had to work with, I didn't blame him for keeping it short and sweet. Niles sat down, and people smiled, impressed that he was able to put the three hard words into a story that fit the narrative. They were grateful. I'm sure many of us will remember his story the next time we buy or eat an apricot.

*****

CH 13 Conches-en-Ouche

"I'm going to change things up a bit," I announced, standing in the aisle of the bus. "We have two gentlemen up here on my right and two ladies up here on my left. Rather than ask each of them to tell separate stories, I'm going to ask each pair to get together and craft a story from *two* slips of paper. This may be easier, or it may be harder; I don't know. I guess we'll find out. Who wishes to go first?"

The men raised their hands quickly, so I went over to the first man sitting closest to the aisle. "And you are?"

"I'm Watkins," he said, "I'm a journalist."

"Oh, so we have a ringer in our midst, do we?" said the shop-owner lady who had told a story earlier.

"I guess we do," I answered, "but who is teaming up with him?"

"I'm Amherst," said the man nearest the window, "I'm a photographer."

"Oh, so you're the one who gave us those reference words about photos, right?" I asked.

He nodded.

"Very good. Well, I think you two should be able to knock this one out of the park. Let's all take notes; perhaps we can write a book on this when we get back."

Watkins laughed as he took a piece of paper from the hat. Amherst followed, opening his quickly and putting it down. They began talking before we could find out what their words were, but that wasn't a problem. I just waited, and when they were ready, I prompted them.

"And your words are?" I asked.

"He's got *Atom, Red*, and *Math*," said Watkins.

Before turning to the physicist, I said, "I'm sure you can thank Jansen here for his contribution."

Jansen only smiled in reply.

"And I've got *Bobby, Crime,* and *Rain*," Watkins continued.

"This could be tougher than I thought," I said to the group. "But if anyone is up to the challenge, it should be the two of you. So, what do you have for us?"

"Once upon a time ..." Watkins began cheekily. People on the bus laughed before he continued. "Our orders were changed, and Lieutenant Jack told us the news.

"'We're being sent east,' he said. 'The Canadians have been ordered north and the Americans south. We're all pushing toward Paris and the Seine. Our objective now is to take Evreux, which is south of Rouen and north of Chartres. We will be accompanied by other corps from the British Second Army so we won't be on our own during this part of our mission. So, saddle up. We have more work to do.'

"It was about that time when the wind and rain came. Fall was fast approaching, and we could feel the chill in the air. Perhaps it was just an omen, but if it was, it was a bad one. Something in my bones told me new blood would be shed in the coming days.

"I hurried to the lieutenant and asked him why we were being ordered east."

"'I don't know,' he answered. 'Those are the orders, and we gotta follow them.'

"'Yes, sir, but it doesn't add up. Why wouldn't we continue south to take the rest of France first and then swing back up to squeeze Paris?'

"I don't do the math, sergeant. I only do what I'm told. The generals - Monty, Bradley and Eisenhower know what they're doing. I've got faith in them. You have to as well. That's what war is about. You take your orders and you follow them the best you can. As a lieutenant I can make a few decisions on the ground, but when it comes to the big stuff, they're in charge. They've got their intel and their big maps. All we have are two eyes and two ears. We can only see and hear what's within seeing and hearing distance. You follow me?'

"I saluted my lieutenant and fell back into formation – following orders.

"We pressed ahead into a town called Conches-en-Ouches -- a place I'll never forget. As we approached the town, a shot rang out – just one, single shot. I looked back to see what the lieutenant's order was.

"'Lieutenant?' I asked, 'what do you ...' but that's when I stopped. Lieutenant Jack slumped over onto me and then dropped to the ground. I grabbed him and turned him over. The blood drained from my head and I squatted to keep from falling myself. The bullet had gone directly through his forehead, making a small entrance wound, but massive exit one. He was dead. On the ground next to him was his book on apricot trees that had fallen out of his backpack. I picked up his body and carried it to the side of the road where we all got down.

"'A sniper,' said Marvin, my corporal. 'One shot like that from that far from the town. It's got to be a sniper.'

"'A crime ... it's just a crime,' I said.

"'Yeah, it's awful. They say the best sniper can almost shoot a single atom out of the sky bind-folded,' said the corporal.

"Even though every death is a tragedy, I felt more loss from the death of our lieutenant. He, like all the men I knew who were killed on that campaign, was a good man. I didn't get to know him well, but well enough that I knew the world would miss him."

"'What do we do now?' asked Brandon, one of the young privates.

"'I don't know,' said Luke, one of the few left from my original platoon. He looked at me and added, 'but you're our CO now, sergeant. Our platoon doesn't have a second lieutenant, so you're it.'

"Suddenly, I realized he was right. As sergeant, I had been thrown into the role of commanding officer whether I liked it or not. Under me, I had three corporals, a lance corporal, and five privates. Not exactly a precinct of bobbies, but also not a strong show of force. Without asking, I knew we wouldn't be getting another CO - not this late in the campaign. But, there was one thing I could do.

"I took my lieutenant's walkie-talkie and called the major in charge of our company. I explained the situation, and he gave me a chilling reply: 'Take him out.'

"'What?' I had asked, the first time talking with a major.

"'Take him out!' shouted the major, *'Kill the god-damned sniper!* Those are your orders.' Then, the line disconnected."

"'Well, what did he say?' asked my first corporal, Sam."

"'He said to terminate the sniper,' I answered, with a blank look on my face. 'I guess we've got more work to do, eh?'"

"'How the bloody hell are we supposed to do that?' asked my corporal. 'Snipers are the hardest damned targets to kill – even by other snipers!'

"'I guess that's for us to figure out,' I answered.

"Conches-en-Ouches was directly ahead of us, less than two kilometers. Yet, within that small town there was a stealthy killer that had to be taken out. Normally, I would have hesitated going after such a highly-trained marksman, but in this case, it was personal to me. He had killed my lieutenant, and I wanted vengeance.

"My map was too general to help me with the small town that hid the killer. So, we were on our own. Crossing the small river they called Le Rouloir that bordered on the west side of town, we cautiously approached the town. The shops were closed and shuttered as if there had been a national holiday that day. Yet, that was too simple and too easy. No, this was a national emergency like France had never seen before.

"'How the hell are we going to find this guy?' asked Art, my field gunner.

"'It won't be easy,' I answered, 'It's like trying to shoot at a grain of sand that's blowing in the wind. Except in this case, it's nighttime for us.'

"'… and the moon isn't even out,' added Art.

"I just nodded, solemnly.

"That night we found an abandoned storefront and bunked inside, but kept our sentries on watch, rotating shifts throughout the night. It wouldn't be until morning that we'd resume our hunt for the elusive sniper who had felled our CO.

"That morning, all we could do was watch, listen and talk to those townspeople who could or would tell us about anyone or anything that was suspicious in the town, now that the German forces had largely retreated. But, after several worthless discussions, we found one person who gave us a clue.

"'Perhaps,' said the shopkeeper, who owned a dry-goods store near the wooded area in the center of town. He spoke with Luke, our French interpreter. 'I've seen someone up near the church. He's not a parishioner of ours as I go there now that the Germans have left the town. He doesn't wear a German uniform though. But he does speak unusually good German – fluent in fact. I've wondered about him for the past several days. I see him in town, but I sense that he doesn't belong here. Do you know what I mean?'

"There was a older woman, perhaps from the same parish, who told us something similar. 'He's a loner,' she said. 'He's very intense and focused. I see him at night walking in the streets and going into abandoned buildings around town. He carries a case, but I don't know what's in it. That could be who you are looking for.'

"There were two more assassinations while we were searching for the sniper -- another lieutenant and a major from our company -- both killed as their troops approached the city.

"We had little time left to find and eliminate the German threat, and I decided to stake out the one place that seemed to hold the key for us: Eglise Sainte-Foy. It was an old abbey, built in the eleventh century that stood high in the center of town. With its tall towers, it would be the ideal place for a marksman to setup shop and pick-off British officers at long-range. Even with that, I realized that snipers usually move to different locations. Yet, that position was just too good to pass up for a sniper. *He would be back*, I thought. *And when he does, I'll be waiting.*

"That day we waited - all spread out, hiding inside various buildings that surrounded the abbey. It was impossible, though, to figure out who was a worshipper and who was a killer. Even a sniper would have hidden his rifle in the abbey rather than carry it out in the open.

"The hours passed, and all of us found it difficult to keep our focus. I often wondered how snipers could sit in one position for days – unmoving – waiting for just the right target. And even then, be able to pull the trigger within microseconds to kill someone.

"It was just after 1930 hours as the daylight was tumbling toward nightfall when a man entered the church and disappeared inside. He looked almost like every other parishioner, except for one thing: he didn't make the sign of the cross when he passed through the front doors. I immediately ordered my team to surround the building and not let anyone go in or come out.

"Just as we had done at the church outside of Caen, we entered with guns drawn. The priest stopped us and shook his head, telling us in French that we were not welcome there and pointing toward the door. But my corporal, who spoke French, whispered to him that there was a killer among his congregation. Still, the minister only shook his head at us, telling us firmly that *all* who enter his church are, as he said, *'Children of God.'*

"Unwilling to waste any more time, I ordered two of my men up the second tower, while my corporal and I climbed the stairs to the taller one. We were quiet, each taking the two hundred plus steps as quickly but as silently as we could. It was only when we reached the top that we heard a noise.

"I held up my hand for my corporal to stop behind me, pointing upwards to tell him of our target. Then, I raised my pistol to surprise the killer and end his rain of terror. However, instead, I heard the sickening sound of his rifle shooting out a fatal round before I had the chance. That was a sound I will never forget either. It is one of many regrets I still hold in my heart during that mission. Later, I would find out that the bullet killed a sergeant from my company, but another platoon, who was part of a surge group ordered to take the town by force, regardless of the sniper on the loose. Sergeant Tennison never knew what happened. I was told he died instantly.

"However, the sniper heard me from below, and he wheeled around, starting to draw his pistol. This time, it was my bullet that stopped him. The bullet pierced his throat, and he clutched it but then let go, as if he knew he been bested. He looked at me with his piercing brown eyes; however, there was no hatred or enmity. I even think he gave me a slight smile before he died, knowing that someone just as clever had brought his end.

"Doubling over, the German collapsed, his hand twitching as though he wanted one last chance to shoot a Brit. Thank God, I never gave him that chance.

"We withdrew from Conches-en-Ouche, having completed our mission there. I radioed in that the threat had been eliminated, but the major only grunted. 'Move on toward Evreux,' he said. 'You need to be there by dusk.'

"It wasn't that I expected a 'thank you' or a 'good job.' You didn't get those when you were in the heat of battle. Yet, the fact that we were all still alive and no more Brits would fall to that sniper, was gratitude enough."

*****

CH 14 Carrots

I had to take a deep breath after he'd finished. It was as if I'd been there, in the tower, with him – feeling all the emotions and stresses.

"How do you know so much about that?" I asked both of them. "It was almost like you'd been there before."

"I'm a journalist, and he's a photographer," said Watkins. "We just know a lot of stuff between us, I guess. I studied war journalism in college and probably picked up something along the way." He looked at me without really answering the question, but I understood nonetheless.

"Well, nice job," I said. "I think you had me on the edge of my seat most of the time on that one, anyway. Now, where were we? We still have some more papers in here to be plucked. Who wants to follow that nice bit of charming?"

Standing in front of me was a brawny man -- young and handsome. His arms were as big around as my thighs and his square jaw and stubble face suggested he was serious about anything he attempted.

"What about you, sir? What's your name?"

"Peter," he said, surprisingly shyly.

"And what brings you to this lovely part of England with the rest of us?"

"I'm headed to Waterbury to attend a funeral," he said, sadly.

"Oh, I'm very sorry," I answered him. "Is it someone close?"

"It's me brother," he said, his eyes drooping and voice falling. "He died last week. I couldn't be there when he passed. He'd been sick for a while."

"Well, Peter, you don't have to do this. I ... we ... will understand."

"No, I think it may do me some good," he said, looking at me with his big, brown eyes. "Let me have a go."

He put his giant fist inside the hat and pulled out a paper.

94

"It says here ... well ... I can only read two of the words written on it. There's *Truth*, *Cooking*, and ... not sure ... I think it says *Buggars*?"

I looked at the scrap. "Perhaps it's *Beggars*," I said, also unsure.

"Yeah, I think you're right," he answered. "Well, let's see," he began nervously. "We all wanted to get out of that small town as fast as we could, but the sun had already dropped down below the tree-lined forest. Our reinforcements from the rest of the company would be coming in to take over the next morning to secure the rest of the town while we were expected to march on to that E-town," he said looking at me.

"I think we said it was Evreux," I told him.

"Yeah, Evroo," he said, botching the name. "Anyway, we bunked in one of the abandoned, small shops and when we started opening our rations that night, our lance corporal shouted to me that we had a visitor. When I went out to see who it was I was surprised. Standing before me was the most beautiful young woman I had ever seen. She was young and stunning. Her blonde hair and high cheekbones radiated a strength I hadn't seen in a long time. Dressed in a simple, white cotton dress, she carried a tray of pastries that looked like they'd been made at a five-star restaurant. Chocolate eclairs, croissants, Napoleons, and macarons -- all looked delicious.

"The young woman stood in the doorway, nervous, yet yielding a slight smile.

"'Do you like French pastry?' she asked in French.

"Luke, our corporal translator, smiled at me and without interpreting anything answered, '*Oui, oui!*'

I didn't have to know French to understand what they were talking about. I smiled back at her, mesmerized by her beauty. 'Yes,' I said, followed awkwardly by, "*Oui, oui*."

"The pastries looked exquisite. I hadn't had many of the things on her tray, but she was an angel from heaven, bearing such a plate.

"'Well, aren't you going to invite her in?' asked my corporal, waiting for my orders.

95

"'Uh, sure. Yes, of course,' I said, unable to get the smitten grin off my face. I gestured and pointed inside so she knew she was welcome.

"All the gents inside drooled as she entered, and she smiled again as she set the tray in front of us, so we could see what she brought.

"'I have a variety of things for you,' she said. 'We are so grateful that you have come and freed us from the Germans. We can't tell you how happy we are that you are here.'

"'Are you telling me the truth?' I asked, even though I already knew the answer.

"'Oh, of course,' she said, this time surprisingly answering in English. 'The last four years have been hell for everyone here. We have waited a long time for this. Thank you for coming.'

"My troops dug into the pastries like they'd never eaten one before. Everything was devoured in minutes, even though the young girl was there longer.

"'What is your name?' I asked, looking into the most stunning eyes I had ever beheld.

"'I'm Jacquelyn,' she answered. "Do you see anything you like?" referring to the tray.

"'Yes, I must say I do,' I answered, but not in the same way she intended. She didn't catch my intention, but that was fine. Then, I added, 'Do you live nearby? Here in town?'

"'*Oui*,' she said. 'Not far.'

"We sat and talked for a long time. Her story was like others. Her family had been ripped apart by the war. She admitted to me that she was Jewish. Her parents had been taken away when the Germans had come, but she didn't know where. She hadn't heard from them since they'd left. She hadn't been home when the SS agents had come knocking. Her brother had hidden in the basement while his parents denied they had any children at home. The French Underground had gotten her brother out of France, but she had stayed with a friend who had kept her hidden.

"After the pastries and my long talk with her, we said our goodbyes. I would always remember her glowing face and cheerful disposition. It was too bad we didn't have more time together, but that's the way of war, I guess.

"Pushing out of Conche-en-Ouche, we were within striking distance of Evreux. Surprisingly, there was no resistance as we marched into the city. The town was in ruin, though, having been bombed by the Germans when they came into France and then again by the Allies only days earlier to clear the enemy out and force them to evacuate.

"But as we walked down the mostly-deserted streets, we saw beggars outside homes and shops with cups or hats collecting whatever they could from the troops coming to town. Dirty and haggard, the old men had been cast aside - thrown to the curb like human garbage awaiting pickup for the dump. It was a pitiful sight, and it pulled strongly on my heartstrings.

"Yet, soon I heard another small group of people cheering as people began coming out of their homes. We fell into line with other platoons and companies marching down the street. Lining the roadway were more and more people, waving the old French Tricolour – the blue, white and red flag. People were happy, and it was obvious they hadn't felt that way for a long time."

Peter finished and abruptly sat down.

"Very nice," I said. Then I glanced at the gentleman sitting next to him. "Would you be willing to contribute?" I asked.

The man cocked his head with indifference. "If I must," he answered grudgingly.

He read his slip and then sat thinking. He finally told us his words were: *Children, Gardening* and *Happiness.*

I wasn't sure whether he would take up the challenge, but even he surprised me.

"Well …" he began quickly.

"I'm sorry," I said, "I didn't catch your name?"

"Oh, I'm Donald Westcot."

"Donald, very nice to meet you," I answered. "And what do you do, Donald?"

"I'm an architect. I've been one for ... well ... going on forty-three years. A long time, that is."

"Yes, it certainly is. I'm sorry to have stopped you in mid-sentence. As you were saying, Donald ..."

"Yeah, right. Well, the people of Evreux were lovely, and the farther into the city we went the more we saw things that looked more normal. People were going in and out of shops, children were playing in the streets, and even others were sitting outside at the cafe, having a late afternoon coffee or beer. Of course, in those days many people smoked, so the plumes of gray were drifting out the doors of many a shop and cafe all about town. Generally, I would say, the mood was festive and warm.

"As we traveled through the town to the other side, I noticed the small homes near the road and those off in the distance with clothes lines full of patrons – pants, shirts, socks, and other garments fluttering in the wind. At a distance, they looked like tattered flags flapping on the green back lawns of the many small plots. Dogs ran freely in the yards, and I spotted a young lad playing catch with his golden retriever - casting out a stick and waiting for his trusted mate to run and bring it back to him. It was hard to see which of them was having more fun.

"Behind another house was an older woman down on her hands and knees pulling weeds from her garden. It was late in the season, and it appeared she had a good crop of tomatoes, yellow squash, beans, and peas, with the tops of some nice radishes and carrots coming in nicely as well.

"She waved to me as we passed, and I halted my platoon and went to talk with her, taking my corporal to translate. When we got to the fence behind her house, she held out two bunches of carrots she had pulled.

"'Here,' she said in French. 'Take them. You boys look like you could use some fresh vegetables.'

"I smiled and thanked her, reaching in my pocket to give her something for them, but she shook her head. 'No, no,' she answered. 'Please. Take them. It is my pleasure to do this for you.'

"We went back to the rest of the guys and handed out the carrots. They were fresh and crunchy, and she was right, I was starved for some fresh vegetables – something I thought I would never say. And wouldn't you know, those were the best damned carrots I'd ever eaten in my life, too. That, my friends, is what true happiness feels like.

"And that's all I got," said Donald, finishing his part of the tale with efficiency and exactitude.

"All right, then," I said, nodding his way. I looked into the hat. There were still a few pieces of paper left as not everyone had taken a turn. "Come on," I barked, "some of you have yet to jump in. None of us on this bus bites, after all. Come on!"

"All right," moaned another bus passenger. "If I must."

This would be a part of the tale I would also remember for a long time to come.

*****

CH 15 Enlightenment

I looked down at the man and was surprised that I hadn't noticed him before. He was rather unremarkable – plain, really. He was small-framed, and bespectacled. His glasses were simple, black-framed, ovals that didn't suggest any occupation or flair. Dressed in a light-gray sweater with a brown and black plaid shirt beneath and a pair of black, twill pants, his hand shook as he pulled out the small shapes from the hat.

I waited patiently as he read the form. "What is your name?" I asked.

"Niles, Niles Jacobson," he said, looking up. Then, he added, "I'm with the Ministry of Foreign Affairs."

He said nothing more and plopped his piece of paper back into the hat. I panicked, looking down into the layer of remaining white slips to figure out which one he had picked. I pulled one out and read it aloud.

"Was this the slip?" I asked, handing it to him.

He glanced at it and moaned. "Yes," he answered, "I got *Color*, *Essence*, and *Renoir*."

It was then I understood why he had thrown the piece back into the hat. "My apologies," I said without thinking.

"Why are you apologizing?" he asked, blinking aimlessly.

"I … I don't know. I'm not sure. I guess the words you have to work with are … well … a little harder than …"

"Yes, yes," he said again, "it's no problem. I'm a trained professional. I can handle this – actually, I can handle most anything."

He pushed back the long, thick locks that were covering his forehead and cleared his throat. "Where were we?" he asked, as if bored by the entire process.

"I believe the troops were just leaving the small town of Evreux," I said.

"Happiness, yes," said the man, "that's where we were. I believe everyone should be happy, of course. So, as we left Evreux we all felt better about things – about life and about the future. However, we would soon realize that we had nothing for which to be so sanguine."

"Sanguine," I repeated, impressed with his vocabulary.

Niles only rolled his eyes at me. "Anyway, we continued our march. Lacking enough supplies and weapons – starved of these by our own government which refused to open the purse strings to our needs – we trudged to our next mission. The road now inevitably turned toward Paris. Between us and that large city was Mantes-la-Jolie, a medium-sized town that was supposed to have been abandoned by the Nazis. Our small company was sent there to join-up with other troops and, as I recall, the French Forces of the Interior or FFI. But, as we found later, it was only our company in Mantes-la-Jolie – only our company of one hundred against a brigade of nearly five thousand Germans.

"I remember it being August, and the color of the leaves on the trees along the countryside had not yet turned even though fall was approaching. It was nice to have five platoons joining together to form a larger group – most all of us felt more secure knowing there were more rifles available for a shoot-out. What we all wished for, however, were a few Cromwell tanks, clanking alongside us to add more firepower.

"It was a quick day's march, and we reached a broad, serpentine river that snaked through the golden fields and pastoral lands of northern France. It had not rained in days, and the water level was low, exposing shoreline rocks and debris along its boundaries.

"'What do you make of that?' asked Max, one of the privates in our platoon.

"'What do you mean?' I asked him, marching next to him.

"'That river there. Which one is that, now?'

"'I think that's the Seine, if my map is correct,' I answered. I was in charge of my platoon, but I still reported to the larger, company commander, Major Briggs.

"'Oh, that's the one that goes through Paris, right?' he asked. 'It's the one with that Iffel Tower thing. I've always wanted to see that,' said Max, chewing on a blade of barley that was hanging precariously out of his mouth.

"'That's the one,' I said, 'but it's called the Eiffel Tower. They built that back in the 1800s for the world fair. 1889, I think.'

"'Yeah, I really want to see that one. They say it's huge – taller than Big Ben, I hear.'

"'What part of England are you from?'

"'I'm from Halifax, sir,' said the soldier.

"'… good part of the country, Halifax. I've always felt that Manchester and Leeds were the heart of the British people – not London.'

"'Quite right, sir,' said Max. 'So, sergeant, where are we going now?'

"'I don't know exactly, private, but I think we're headed to Paris. There are a few small towns along here before we get there, though. I'm told we shouldn't see much fighting, so I think this part of the mission should be easy.'

"I walked and watched the water as it flowed in the opposite direction we were going. Overhead flew a black-headed sea gull, while three cormorants and a majestic, gray heron waded along the riverbed.

"Soon the river meandered off, disappearing to the east as we continued down the road south toward Paris. But we weren't even to the outskirts of Mantes-la-Jolie when the peace was shattered. Exploding only meters away was a tank round, presumably from a German Panzer stationed just north of the city limits. The shrapnel took out six men in less than a second. Also wounded were Max and myself, although mine were mere scrapes on my upper arm and shoulder. Max went down – a piece of metal severing leg below the knee.

"I rushed to his side and ripped off a piece of my shirt, tying a tourniquet to stop the bleeding. He screamed in pain, his face contorted with the shock of what had just happened. Beside the six dead bodies all around me, there were two others in bad shape being attended to by Luke and Marvin, my corporals.

"But since the round had found its mark so quickly, other rounds followed, and the rest of the company quickly found shelter where they could find it. Exploding all around us were tank shells, blowing craters in the landscape which had lain untouched for centuries.

"I dragged Max into the woods, leaving behind his mangled limb behind, and waited for my orders. Jason, our radio operator, was close by, and we hoped air support would be called in to help. But instead of British planes, there were two Messerschmidt fighters that came in low, trying to strafe us from the air. The machine guns ripped through the wooded forest, shearing bark off trees and forcing a rain of branches and twigs down upon us. The loud roar of their motors faded as the planes' propellers pulled them high into the sky to bank for another pass.

"'My leg!' shouted Max, in total agony. 'They've blown off me leg!'

"I looked on as my private and friend began to fade – shock overcoming his small, slight body frame. 'Hang in there, Max. You've got to stay strong! The medic will be over to see you as soon as he can.'

"'I ain't gonna make it, sir. I … I …'

"I took his wrist and felt for his pulse. It was weak and thready. There wasn't much time for him.

"Another round of shells blasted around us, but the rest of the company began advancing on the German positions. My radio operator said British Spitfires were on their way, but that's not what showed up. Instead, it was the Americans with a squadron of P-51 Mustang fighters that began chasing the 109s out of the sky.

"After a few minutes, the medic finally came running over to our position carrying his black, leather bag. 'How's he doing?' asked the medic, a young man who looked like he was fresh out of training.

"I looked down at Max. I already knew the answer but had to force myself to confirm it. His eyes were glassy and open, unblinking. He was gone.

"'Sorry, mate,' I said, shutting his eyes.

"The medic patted me on the shoulder but said nothing. Instead, he moved quickly to the next casualty. Meanwhile, my company was moving out, and I was forced to leave Max behind for others to care for.

"The battle waged on, with the Americans dropping bombs and the Nazi's retreating. The panzers were pulled out of the town as the American troops converged with the Brits to move into Mantes-la-Jolie. Machinegun nests were thick throughout the city, attempting to slow our advance toward Paris. But that is not what I remember about the town. What I recall vividly is that by the time we arrived, the town had been leveled by bombs. All were flattened by Allied bombing after the invasion at Noland T.dy – all except the church.

"Sitting high above the bank of the Seine sits the red-tiled roof of the grand, city church. With its flying buttresses, it looked like a prototype version of the Cathedral of Notre Dame. Its twin towers soared into the air above the city with the dignity and power of the Roman Catholic religion, brought to the country nearly two thousand years earlier. They called it a church, rather than a cathedral, and it was named the Collegiate Church of Notre Dame. I believe it was built in the twelfth century, at about the same time when Notre Dame de Paris was begun.

"The fighting took several days, but eventually we controlled the town. I recall finally being able to go into the church, opening the massive front doors and walking directly into the nave. The church had been damaged but not seriously, and I found a pew inside. I was not particularly religious, but there was something about that church that penetrated the hard crust of my soul.

"I knelt and made the sign of the cross, even though I was not Catholic. Closing my eyes, I prayed for the first time in months. At first, I thought someone or something was whispering in my ears, but when I opened my eyes I found no one there but the swirling breeze and roiling spirals of dust and debris from the destruction outside.

"As I was leaving, I noticed a small woman, wearing heavy wool clothing and with a thick, dirty, plaid scarf wrapped around her head. Beside her was a small child, also dirty and disheveled. I assumed it was a grandmother with her daughter's child, and then I wondered why the mother was not there too. All I could assume was that the small girl's mother was dead – possibly killed in the bombing or killed when the Germans first seized the town four years earlier.

"I wished I had brought Luke along to interpret for me, but then again, I thought it better not to know. There were too many tragic stories from the war, and I wasn't prepared to learn of another. Rather than tales of heroism, courage and victory, the essence of the war also seemed to include stories of horror, tragedy, and loss."

"After Mantes-la-Jolie, we marched on to the impressive city of Paris. I had been to London a few times before the war, but I hadn't recalled it being nearly as large as Paris. Spreading out in all directions, the city was all that I imagined it to be. While the Germans had conquered the city proper, it had not managed to change its people, culture and uniqueness.

"Lining the streets were throngs of people waving Americana and British flags, smiling and clapping for us. The American troops were there too, parading up the tree-lined Champs Elysees. This, too, was happiness. Virtually untouched by the travesties of the war machine, the city was beautiful – just as it had been before the Germans seized it. We only learned later that the Germans had planned to blowup the town if the Allies threatened to take it back. Thank goodness that never happened.

"Of all the things I wanted to do in Paris, the most important was to go to the Louvre Museum. I was not cultured in that way, but I had always wanted to see the Mona Lisa by Michelangelo. Smaller than what I expected, it was still extraordinary and something I will never forget. Also in the museum were the works of Renoir, Rembrandt, Caravaggio, and others. There were French soldiers guarding all the priceless works, and I wasn't able to get very close; yet, their detail, vivid colors, and historical significance left a lasting impression on me.

"The war would never leave me, even though I left it years ago. Those of us who were there would remember nearly every moment for as long as we would live. It was an era that would change the world forever, and would change every man, woman and child who lived with it forever too. They say wars leave physical scars, but it's the mental ones that are the hardest to heal. Some, in fact, never go away."

Niles ended his long story and sat down. There was silence in the bus as we all absorbed what he had said.

*****

CH 16 Paris Redux

The people on the coach were starting to get restless, regardless of how good the stories were that were told. Everyone wanted to get to their destinations, and it was becoming increasingly hard to keep their attention. The hour was approaching midnight, and we were still waiting for someone to pass by and give us a helping hand. No one since the drunk driver had passed in over an hour, and we were all getting frustrated. Yet, I did my best to keep things moving.

"I hope someone finds us soon," I said, looking at my watch. "We're about out of scraps in this old hat. So, who wants to go next? There are only a few of you left who haven't contributed."

"I'll go," said a woman in front. Yet, the fellow next to her raised his hand at the same time. Being a gentleman, he smiled graciously and put his hand down, gesturing to her to go first.

"Why don't you both go?" I said. "Just like we did a few times earlier, you both can draw and then craft a story from the two scraps. How's that?"

Both nodded and pulled their pieces straight away.

"Now, I know one of you is a painter. We established that earlier," I said, motioning to the woman. "And the other is a …?"

"I'm an author," said the middle-aged gentleman. "I'm going to see my niece in Waterbury. She has two young boys, and I told her I would stay for a few days to visit."

"Nice," I said. "And your name is?"

"I'm Stephen," he answered.

"And I'm Clara," said the painter, putting her hand to her chest. "I'm going to Waterbury to do some painting, actually. There are some marvelous castles and landscapes down there. Of course, they won't rival Renoir, but hopefully they'll turn out."

"So, what are your words?" I asked.

"It appears they are: *Structure, Anger, Creativity* and *Tennis, Money, Success*," said Clara, uncomfortable with all the words.

Even I cringed at the draw. *"Eww,"* I said. "Well, perhaps it's good that you're working together. Talk for as long as you need and then let us know what you come up with."

But the two chatted only for a moment before Stephen started. "I guess we're going to do our own thing with whatever words we come up with," he said. "So, let's see what happens."

Stephen smiled and began.

"Leaving the wonders of Paris behind, we were ordered to get to Calais. The men in my platoon showed up at the rendezvous point angry that they had such little time to spend for R&R in the magnificent city, but when they learned that we were shipping out to England that anger turned to joy.

"'That's the spirit!' said Luke, by now one of my best friends. He lofted a Steiner of beer in a Calais bar the night we were to fly out. All of my platoon was there, and let's just say, we enjoyed the evening.

"'You don' think we had spirit before this?' I yelled back at him from across the wooden table. By this time, we had all gone through four rounds and were well into our fifth.

"'Not a pansy-ass like you,' Luke yelled, standing up. He grinned and winked at me, knowing it would be one of the last times he could take a good-natured jab at me before we got back to England.

"'Pansy ass? Really? That's the best you got?' I said back to him, laughing. 'Sounds to me like it took a pansy-ass to come up with pansy ass in the first place.'

"With that the entire table burst out in laughter, snorting and hooting at the both of us.

"It was Max who pounded his pint and stood up. 'I want to make a toast.' He raised his beer in the air and said, 'I want to make a toast to …'

"'You already, bloody-well said that,' I said, laughing.

"'Okay, okay,' Max answered, trying again. 'Here's to … damn … I forgot what I was going to say, now.'

"Again, the table burst out in laughter.

"'Sit down, then!' yelled Marvin, our corporal in the bunch.

"It was Luke who stood up again. 'I propose a toast to success, prosperity, and to making lots of money when we get back!'

"'Here, here!' shouted everyone at the table, taking another swig.

"'What are you gonna do when you get back, Sarg?' asked Jason, our radio operator.

"'I'm gonna get with my girl, a course,' I said. 'I haven't seen her in years … well months anyway. It seems like years to me.'

"It was then that my mates began making obscene gestures to me, suggesting what I was going to do with her once we were together again.

"Again, I laughed, shrugging it off. All I would say is 'Maybe?'

"The roar from the table began drawing attention from others in the bar, and I quickly put my hands out face down, motioning for them to quiet a bit so we wouldn't be thrown out.

"'What about the rest a ya?' I asked. 'What are you doing when you get home?'

"'I'm ridin' me motorcycle,' said Luke, his eyes glazing over. 'Every time I see one of our majors or colonels ridin' around on one over here, I'm jealous.'

"'Yeah, me too,' said Brandon. 'Except I gotta go get it back from my Uncle Herman. He's been using it while I've been gone. It's a Ducati, and I'm sure he's been riding it into the ground. I'm sure the tires are bald by now, and he's not the kind to change them for me.'

"'I don't have a motorcycle, but my '35 Acedes 16/66. It's a bute. It's got a 1990 cc, three-carburetor engine that puts out over 66 brake-horsepower! Man, does she fly!'

"'Does she have an overhead cam?' asked Sam.

"'Absolutely! She's a well-oiled machine, that she is. She's my baby.'

"'Well, let's just hope none of the rest of us finds that our wives or girlfriends have had any of those while we've been gone!' I said jokingly. 'It has been over nine months since we shipped out, ya' know!'

"Again, there was laughter all around.

"The night wore on until the wee hours of the morning, and the next day came quickly. Structure and order were once again restored, as my entire platoon reported to the airfield just outside of Calais for our trip home.

Stephen glanced over at Clara, who looked surprised that he ended his part of the story so abruptly.

"Oh, does that mean it's my turn?" she asked.

"That's all I have. Sorry to disappoint," said Stephen, suspecting that she thought his session lacked color or excitement.

"Oh, no. I didn't mean it that way," she answered. "I thought it was wonderful. And what was even better, you used four of the six words. All I must do is figure out how to incorporate Tennis and Creativity into the conversation." Then, dryly she added, smiling, "Thanks a lot!"

"It was indeed, excellent, Stephen. I enjoyed it immensely. Now, it's Clara's turn. Clara?"

Clara stood and straightened her wool jacket before she undertook the next stage of the tale's journey.

"The flight back to London was quicker and slightly easier than what we had experienced coming over. There were no machine gun nests or German tanks shooting meter-long shells at us. The bullets weren't screaming overhead so thick that they looked like clouds of mosquitos flying in a straight line, but faster than nature could allow. No, the occasional bump in the airstream was calm compared with that, and that was just fine with us.

"Yet, on the other hand, we were sad. Me mates meant the world to me. We were brothers – we had become family. It was a special bond that we could never explain to anyone who hadn't been through an experience like that. If someone were to write about it without being in the war, it would take a great deal of creativity to pull that off, and few could.

Clara paused – happy that she had at least conquered one of the two difficult words on her list.

"The landing was rough – the plane bouncing on the runway as if it had met a trampoline instead of cement. We all suspected it was a young, novice pilot who was not yet ready for combat duty. I spotted a few in the platoon crossing themselves and looking skyward as the plane finally settled and taxied toward the hangar.

"They rolled the long, metal stairs over to the door in back and hurried us to disembark.

"'We've got six more flights just like this one today gents,' said the less-than-attractive female attendant hurrying us off the plane. 'Let's get off as soon as possible. That means *now!*'

"We dragged our duffels off with us, scurrying down the stairs and hoping that we'd be met by our girls or family. My girl didn't disappoint. She was there, smiling and waving like there was no tomorrow. Me mum was right beside her, beaming as I got off the stairs.

"We had to line up once more, in formation, and wait for our sup to inspect our platoon. After a once-over, the major stood before us at attention and gave us a brisk salute. Not wanting to keep us long, he merely said, 'Good work, men. Dismissed.'

"All of my men ran for their loved ones. I grabbed my girl and kissed her like I'd never kissed a woman in my life. Her lips were warm and inviting. Her skin was soft and her perfume intoxicating. I was glad to be home.

"After that, I gave me mum a big hug and kissed her on the cheek. 'Hi mum,' I said lovingly. 'I missed ya' ya' know.'

"'What about me?' asked Mona, my girlfriend.

"'I'll deal with you later,' I answered, grinning and giving her an impish wink.

"'Okay, you two. No hanky-panky, now. Not until after you're married,' said me mum.

"'Where's Pops?' I asked, looking around for my old man.

My dad wouldn't have missed greeting me at the airport for the world, so it was strange that he wasn't there. My mum looked down at the black asphalt on the tarmac, and it was then that I knew something was wrong.

"'Where's Pops?' I asked again, this time with a higher-pitched voice that signaled I really didn't want the answer.

"I took Mona by the shoulders and forced her to look at me. 'What's wrong?'

"Mona looked at me mum, and when she couldn't get a response, she said, trembling, 'He died suddenly. Just last week. We couldn't tell you – not when you were coming home all happy. Anyway, you wouldn't have gotten the telegram in time. I'm sorry.'

"I stood stunned, finding that my joy had completely evaporated. The shock took me to my knees, and I found myself pounding the pavement. Tears began to flow, but I quickly wiped them off my face and regained my composure. 'I don't understand. He was in great shape. He's never been sick a day in his life. What … what happened?'

"'Doctors said that he had a massive heart attack. He just fell over dead while he was working on the truck outside. Your mum found him.'

"Me Mum began sobbing, taking out a white handkerchief and wiping her eyes. 'I'm sorry, son. I … I didn't know how to tell you. It all happened so fast.'

"I put my arms around her and brought her close. 'It's all right, mum. It's okay. He was a good man. He took care of us, didn't he?'

"She nodded, and together we walked out to the parking lot where we climbed into the old, black, beaten-up Austin sedan and drove home."

Clara started to sit down, but then rose again, putting her index finger into the air to suggest she wasn't quite finished with her story.

"Three weeks passed, and I was still trying to adjust to civilian life. I thought about re-enlisting, but Mona was adamant about setting a wedding date and getting on with our lives. She had waited too long and told me that it was, quote 'now or never.' I decided with her gentle urging that *now* was as good of time as any.

111

"Yet, it was then, that I received an urgent telegram. Opening it, I read quickly, letting my eyes scan the contents to get a gist of what had happened. In those days, one didn't get a telegram unless something big happened. Unfortunately, more times than naught it was something bad. In this case, it was.

> Dear Troy,
>
> It's hard for me to tell you this, but our friend and buddy Luke was killed in a motorcycle accident yesterday. How can it be that he survived D-day and some of the worst fighting during the war, and was killed by a drunk on the road just outside of Liverpool.
>
> I used to believe in God, but now I'm not so sure.
>
> Contact me when you can. It would be great to hear from you.
>
> Your bud for life,
>
> Marvin.

"And so it was true. What the war was unable to take from us, someone in our own country did. I wanted to find the son-of-a-bitch who'd done this, but Mona told me to let it go. 'Anger will only destroy you,' she said. I knew she was right.

"The next years of my life were some of the best I remember. Mona and I had a family – two daughters and a son – and three English setters. We celebrated when the Allies rode into Berlin and took the city in 1945. I believe it was 7 May when the Germans surrendered unconditionally to the Allies and to General Eisenhower, the Supreme Allied Commander. It was over.

Now, Clara sat down. She had finished the tale. Yet, instead of cheering, there was quiet in the bus. Everyone understood the toll those years had taken on the British people and its society. Those were difficult times – some of the most difficult ever experienced in the world. Some survived, many didn't. Yet, for those who did, it was time to move on.

*****

CH 17 The Meaning

I stood in the middle of the bus holding the cap. All I could think of was how the next person would be able to continue the story.

"I don't know who's left," I said. "I've lost track."

"I think this lady over here hasn't taken her turn yet," said Mildred, the older lady sitting in the front of the bus. She didn't point – she didn't have to. Everyone knew to whom she was referring.

"I don't care to participate in your little folly," said the attorney, going back to a book she was reading. "And anyway," she murmured, "I hope Ms. Clara knows that she missed a word."

"Oh, really? I hadn't noticed," I remarked.

"Yes. She excluded *tennis* from her story."

"I believe you're right. However, I will not punish or give her demerits for the omission, if it's alright with you. I think she did very well with the words she had. Anyway, I am curious as to what you're reading. Is it anything good?"

"Nothing you would understand," she answered with snippy sarcasm.

I was expecting to see the title of some serious tome, like *Leviathan* by Hobbes or *The Social Contract* by J.J. Rousseau. Each are at opposite ends of the spectrum with regard to the nature of man, but I thought perhaps she might be, at least, intellectually curious. But, I was wrong.

I smiled as I saw her try to hide the book from view but not before I spotted the title: *The Chronicles of Narnia*, by C.S. Lewis. While a great book, it was not the hard-hitting, intellectual read I expected. Most teenagers have read it before entering high school.

"Well, let's not waste any more time on this, shall we," I said, moving on down the aisle. "There must be someone else who has not yet contributed," I added.

Yet, no one said a word. The bus was silent.

So, I knew I had to complete the saga on my own. Somehow, I felt I owed it to Manny who had left us so abruptly, but who I knew would make good on his word to get us help.

"Well, I guess it's my turn again, unless someone else wants to jump in for a repeat performance."

However, as I suspected, I got no one to volunteer.

"All right then. Where were we? I think we were all back in England after the war, so that's where I'll begin.

"The year was 2005 ..." I said, "... some sixty years after the war ended. A lot had happened in my life between those times. I had married Mona, had four children with her. Each of them had families, and we could count twelve grandchildren amongst that gaggle. And finally, we had just had twin great-grandchildren – born to our middle-daughter's son who had recently gotten married. Indeed, our clan was expanding like wild flowers on a mountainside; we were certainly proud.

"As for me, I went on to be a successful lawyer," I said, now looking directly at the woman on the coach who had refused to help with the story. "Working in London, our firm specialized in civil and criminal cases. I was successful, working my way up the ladder to partner and making plenty of money. We lived in a nice part of London, belonged to the *tennis* club," I stressed, again looking at the attorney, "and had nice cars, took nice vacations, etcetera, etcetera ... everything was going very well for us.

"But there was something missing, and I couldn't put my finger on it. I finally contacted the two remaining buddies from my platoon to see how they were doing. Marvin, a corporal in our platoon, had become a general manager for a plant that made auto parts. He too had gotten married shortly after the war and had a family that was scattered throughout England and, ironically, Germany. He had retired and was living in, of all places, Paris. It is odd how life sometimes brings you full circle with your past. Then there was Jason, our radio operator. He had gone on to work in the growing industry of computers and computer science. He had gotten his college diploma, and he too, had retired in Waterbury."

Even I had to laugh at my own attempt at humor.

"I contacted each, and it only took a few minutes to re-connect. Those bonds of war are just too strong to forget or to break, I guess. I asked each how his life was going, and we ended up corresponding regularly.

"A few more years passed, and by then we were all well into our eighties.

"'Why don't we all go to Paris for a reunion?' Marvin had asked. At that time, he was living on the Left Bank.

"'I think that's a splendid idea, if I can get my grandson to take me,' I had quipped. 'At least he can still read a map without coke-bottle glasses attached to his head.'

Those on the bus laughed.

"So, we planned to meet in Paris for a reunion, albeit just the three of us. I had learned from some research and inquiry, that we three were, indeed, the last surviving members of our platoon. It had been sixty-four years since we had seen each other. So, on June 6 of that year, we met at a small café just off the Champs-Elysees, fittingly called Café Libération.

"Marvin was already sitting at a table he had reserved for us, sipping an espresso. When he saw me, he rose and smiled, extending his hand eagerly. At first, I didn't recognize him. It was true that he had sent a photo so we might have some chance of acknowledging each other, but seeing him in his decrepit state only made me reflect on my own condition. I wasn't in much better shape.

Marvin was hunched over with a severe spinal condition. He was able to keep his head upright, but his thick spectacles and nearly bald held made him look feeble and frail. Long gone was the bold, strong chest and thick biceps. Instead, he trembled slightly as he extended his hand – a sign of early Parkinson's I suspected.

"'My friend, how are you?' I asked, greeting him.

"'As well as can be expected at our age,' he answered.

"'Have you heard from Jason?

"'Yes, he said he was running a few minutes late, but that he would be here.

"'It's been too long, my friend,' I said. 'You know we can't wait sixty-odd years to do this again, don't you?'

"We laughed and had a seat. It was no more than a moment later when Jason found us, and we greeted him the same way.

"Jason was not in as bad of shape as Marvin, and I regret to admit, he was in better shape than I. He was able to stride into the café with a gait that was slower than in 1944, but quicker than I had expected. Still tall but more lanky and angular than I had recalled, he was smiling and as jocular as ever. Life had been good to him, and it was obvious that his family genes had also contributed to his late-life spryness.

"Of course, we all had changed. No longer young and fit, we were shorter and either grayer or balder than before. However, I believe, we were also wiser. Not only had we changed, but the times had changed as well. Lifestyles were freer and easier. Technology had made many things simple and other things hard. It had sped up our lives immensely, causing us either panic and frustration or awe and wonder.

"But, with all the change, many things had remained static. And as we talked about what was happening in the world, we realized that some things had not changed at all. There was still violence. There were still despots who wanted to do terrible things to people. There was still all of that. And deep inside me, I wondered if those things would ever change. *Will the youth of today still be talking about such things sixty years from now?* I thought.

"'Do you think about the war now?' I asked the other two. 'Clearly, it was worth fighting, otherwise, we might be speaking German and living in labor camps.

"'Not a day passes that I don't think about it,' said Marvin. 'As a young man, it leaves an indelible impression on you. It's something you can never shake-off.'

"'He's right,' said Jason. 'I'm not sure I ponder it every day, but I certainly reflect on it. I still have nightmares about the snipers, the machine gun nests, and getting across the beach without getting my arms blown off. Yeah, I do think about those things.'

"'Do you think such a war will ever happen again?' I asked, finishing my espresso.

"'Will the sun rise in the morning?' asked Jason, skeptically. 'Isn't it man's nature to be the warring sort?'

"'I'd like to think not,' I answered.

"'But a hope is not the same as reality, is it?' asked Marvin. "I wish it weren't true, but we're talking frankly here. That's the way I feel.'

"'Well, if it does happen again, the stakes will be a lot higher. We could destroy the earth the next time around. Another world war would probably annihilate everything, don't you think?'

"Everyone nodded in agreement. So, I asked another question. 'What do you think it would take for that *not* to happen? How can we avoid World War III?'

"'I think it would take a bit of sanity,' said Jason, 'and that's something I'm not sure we have anymore. Every time I look around, I find common sense to be thrown out the window. Things make no sense these days. Things that used to be good are now evil; things that used to be evil, are now good. How can that be? We used to have the Bible teachings at my church. Those were the tenants that kept us all in line. We don't have those anymore. People make up what they think is right and just instead of having anything as a bedrock from which to live thie lives. It's become what's convenient for them – what's expedient for them. It's all for them – not for anyone else. They don't bloody-well care what happens to anyone else. It's all about them, now. It's horrible! People get offended by the smallest things, and we must change our society just to accommodate them? Really? We can't speak our minds anymore for fear of being arrested and thrown in jail. That's what they did in the Soviet Union under Stalin and look where that got them? Fifty million dead! We've already had three book burnings this year alone – all at major universities – Cambridge, Oxford, the University of London and the Sorbonne. Our brothers fought and died in the war to make sure Britain remained free, didn't we? We didn't want to be ruled by Germany or anyone else.'

"'It was 1933,' I said, 'when the German Student Union declared war on all literature deemed anti-nationalist, subversive and against what the Nazi party deemed *acceptable* material for public consumption. They burned hundreds of thousands of volumes to suppress free speech and expression. That is why I fought in the war – to fight for our rights to speak our minds and write what we believe. It never meant that others had to read it or listen to it, but it was our right to express it.'

117

"'Yes, Winston would be turning in his grave if he knew what was happening to his beloved England,' said Marvin.

"'Not only England, but the entire world,' I countered. 'He would wonder whether we had actually won or *lost* the war, I imagine.'

"'In some ways, I think we won the battle, but we lost the war after all. Of course, it would have been much worse had Hitler taken England and then, perhaps, America – especially after what the Allies found on the march toward Berlin – the concentration camps and all. I just hope we don't fall to a tyranny like the Soviets endured – where a small group of people decided the fate of millions.'

"'That was another thing Churchill was right about --' I said, ' – Stalin. He never trusted that son-of-a-bitch, and now that we know he murdered twenty million of his own people, Winston has been vindicated.'

"'It seems to me that the pot is still boiling. It's only a matter of time before another Stalin gets control of things. Russians love a ruthless, patriarchal leader, and by god they're about to get another one! Mark my words!' said Jason.

"Eventually, our stories and talk turned to other, more benign subjects.

"'Do you ever think about that girl you met in Evreux?' asked Jason, looking at me.

"I smiled, 'Yes, I guess I do sometimes. But I was very lucky. I found the love of my life before I left for duty, and I was able to return to her. Mona was the best. She was everything to me – she was my life.'

"Marvin reached out and put his hand on mine. 'I was sorry to hear of her passing,' he said, giving me comfort.

"'Yeah, it's been tough. I miss her dearly, you know.' I said, trying to keep my emotions in check.

"'And what about that young woman at the farmhouse? She certainly was a special dish, wasn't she?' asked Jason.

"Marvin gave us a surprised look. 'Ah, I never told you?' he said, smiling. 'Recently, I tracked her down. I made a trip back to that village and found her. She was divorced and still living in the same house her parents had. As sweet as ever, she and I got reacquainted, don't you know. She now lives with me in Paris. Her name is Margaux.'

"'I'll be damned,' I said. 'Nice job, Marvin. We always thought she was a catch.'

"'Is she as beautiful as ever?' asked Jason.

"'Yes, yes. That she is, mate.'

"'I had forgotten that too,' I said, smiling. 'I guess our war years really did have an impact on our lives, didn't it?'

"'I think the war had a huge impact,' said Marvin. 'Anyone who was living at that time can remember where they were when they were told of D-day. Young people today just can't fathom the terror we all had in those days. Of course it was worse for those of us fighting, but our families at home also suffered, didn't they? None of us knew if we were going to win or lose the war– if there would be life after the war for us or not. Whether our lives would return to normal – if we won -- or whether they would be harsh and brutal, like the French found out when the Germans took over in 1940. That's a far cry from getting your feelings *hurt* by someone saying something you didn't found offensive. Back in the 40s it was really life and death. Family and friends *were* dying – killed by bombs falling in London or by having their heads blown off by a German machine gun on the battlefield. That was our reality and it was raw.'

"'Yes, it was,' said Jason. 'It was *too* real. Many came back hollowed shells of their former selves. There was no such thing as PTS syndrome then. You didn't get special shrink sessions at the veterans' hospital. We all had it to some degree – PTS, that is. Should we have gotten treatment? Sure. But if you listen to the whiney-asses of today, it's something we *owe* them – like everything else. We *owe* them this – we *owe* them that. It's pathetic. In our day, you did it out of duty to your country. As the U.S. President Kennedy said in his 1961 Inaugural Address, "Ask not what your country can do for you – ask what you can do for your country."'

"We chatted the rest of the afternoon, and before it was time to go …"

At that moment, I was stopped in mid-sentence as a young man in the middle of the bus stood. His hair was cut short – military style – and he stood rigid and erect.

"Would you like to say something?" I asked him.

He didn't answer, but instead motioned for me to extend the hat one more time. I did without thinking, and when he reached inside, he found there were no more pieces of paper.

"What am I supposed to do now?" he asked, shrugging his broad shoulders.

It was then that the doctor ran up the three steps of the coach from outside. Oddly, it was the first time she had been back inside the bus since the accident.

"I forgot to give you this." She handed me another scrap of paper. "Manny gave this to me before he left. He said he had wanted to put it in the hat but had forgotten."

Rather than put it in the hat, I merely handed it, as folded, to the man standing before me.

"What's your name?" I asked, turning toward him.

"Ari," he answered, reluctantly.

"Ah, Ari. I'm sorry I didn't catch you earlier. What is your profession, Ari?"

"I'm on leave, sir. Part of the British Army, sir."

"And you're headed to Waterbury for …?"

"Me parents live there. I'm stationed up north, you see. I only get a bit of leave, so I wanted to get down to see them. I'm supposed to ship out in two weeks."

"Well, we thank you for your service to our country, Ari. I bet this story really hits home for you then?" I asked.

"Yes, sir," he answered, lowering his head. "It hits home more than you can imagine. I should have spoken up earlier, but I didn't think I had anything to contribute. I haven't seen war, but I can only imagine what those men went through. I'm told it's hell. Well, actually, I'm told it's *worse* than hell, sir. And having been in the same company for more than nine years, I understand how close you get to your buds. I'm a major, sir, and those in my company mean the world to me. They're family, you know. I would lay down my life for them and they would for me. It's just that kind of thing. It's hard to describe, but it's real. When your life is in danger almost every day, every hour, every minute, when you're in the field of battle, you need to be able to rely on somebody. Someone has to have your back, you know? That's what we do. We have each other's backs. As the American movie title said so well, we are a Band of Brothers. If one dies, a little part of all of us dies with him."

"Ari, I think you've already told us your story. You don't have to do this," I said.

"No, I feel part of this group too. I should contribute to the story as well. It's only right."

"Okay. Then, feel free to unfold that last slip. Let us know where the story goes from here."

As he pealed the scrap and read the words, he frowned.

"What are the words?" I asked.

He didn't answer me but only handed me the slip. I read it and smiled.

"What am I supposed to do with this?" he asked.

I shrugged and put my hand on his shoulder. "Tell it from your heart, major. Whatever comes to mind. The floor is yours," I instructed.

"I'm Aaron," he repeated nervously, "but you can call me Ari."

Ari cleared his throat and continued. "Well, my words are: *Meaning*, *Of*, and *Life* – I suppose they mean, What is the meaning of life? That's a pretty hard question to answer. But all I have to do is tell a story with those words in it, right?"

I nodded. "Do your best," I said, encouragingly.

"Okay, so after Paris, I thought a lot about what my friends and I had talked about – the war, our families, the world. And it all boiled down to their life's experiences – what we had shared together and what was important to each of us. Throughout my life, I always wondered what people meant when they asked, 'What is the meaning of life?' I mean, it's a very hard question to answer, isn't it?

"Does it mean how well you've lived your life? Does it mean whether you've made a difference by what you did or didn't do during your life? Does it mean whether you've been good or bad in your life? What does it mean?

"I've seen war. I've seen death and destruction, and I can tell you that war is certainly *not* the purpose of life. Everyone knows that, after all. Yet, when faced with a pure evil that is capable of killing or enslaving millions, there isn't a choice. You must wage war. You must defeat the evil. Evil must not be allowed to survive. It's bad that you must kill others in order to get to and kill the kernel seed of evil. But if you don't, it will hurt others in unspeakable ways.

"What is remarkable and pure is that so many of us put our lives on the line to kill the evil. We were the only thing that stood between Hitler and world domination. If we hadn't stopped him, how many more would have died, and continued to die even now, inside those horrible concentration camps. Millions? Hundreds of millions? Even billions?

"Yet, me and my mates didn't think twice about it. We were willing to sacrifice ourselves to stop the evil. So many families were shattered by the war. So many sons never returned to their mothers and girlfriends or wives and children. So many children went without their fathers – wives without their husbands – mothers without their sons.

"But even though we killed others to kill the evil, wasn't this sacrifice one of our own redemption too? Sure, we killed Germans but wasn't it a noble cause? We deprived the mothers, wives and children of those soldiers the chance to be with their sons, husbands, and fathers too, but wasn't it different somehow?

"I don't know too much history, but I often hear about armies in the distant past saying that they were 'right' because they had God on their side. In most cases, both sides would say the same thing, yet only one would win. Long ago, the winners would slaughter or enslave the losers too. Was that righteous? Was that what God wanted?

"As God-fearing people, we want to do what we think God would want us to do. In the second world war, it was easy – Hitler didn't believe in God, so He couldn't be on the side of the Nazis. I guess that's why I can sleep at night and have for the past sixty some years since the war ended. That doesn't mean that I don't think about it all the time, though. I do, and apparently so do my mates who are still alive anyway. We all think the same thing. If not for us, where would the world be?

"The one thing that does keep me up at night, is not whether we did the right thing. It's whether we have the courage today to do the right thing. I'm told we do – that we would send in the armies to defeat another Hitler if he should rise up again in another form in the world. I would hope so, but how can we be sure? It seems we have many excuses to turn a blind eye to evil when it's not in our own backyard. We give excuses as to why it's acceptable in other parts of the globe. We pardon the behavior of others because they had 'a difficult childhood.' On a bigger scale, governments ignore beastly actions of other countries because it is not in their own 'best' interest. Where is the morality? Where are the principles? Without those, how can we possibly stand up to another Hitler?"

Ari paused, unsure where to go from there. Then, he said, "I returned home from the trip to Paris and found a sealed envelope waiting for me. It was addressed to me with my army rank of those many years ago: Sergeant instead of Mr. I used my pocket knife to cut open the top and slide out the neat, tri-fold inside. Unfolding the missive, I began reading.

> *Dear Sergeant,*
>
> *I'm afraid I wasn't totally honest with you when we were in Paris. It's something that has gnawed at me for decades, and I thought I could bring myself to tell you when we were together, but I just never found the right moment – or chose not to.*
>
> *You see, it has to do with our favorite interpreter, Luke. Remember when I sent you that note about his death? I think I said that he died in a terrible motorcycle accident. He always loved his motorcycle, you know. He talked a lot about it, and we were all envious. I think we all hoped we would get one when and if we got back to England. I imagine some of us did buy a motorcycle when we got back; I don't know.*
>
> *Anyway, I'm writing to tell you that what I wrote to you was what his family wanted everyone to hear. But, he really didn't die in a motorcycle accident. Sarg, Luke killed himself.*
>
> *It's been more than sixty years since his death, and I think his suicide had as much impact on me as the entire war. I'm sorry to tell you this in this way, but … I guess I was a coward after all. I just couldn't find the words.*
>
> *I hope you understand and will forgive me.*
>
> *Forever your mate,*
>
> *Marvin.*

"I sat stunned – unable to think or breathe. How could this have happened? How could he do that? How could he fight through the bloodiest, goriest times of the war and end up killing himself?"

Ari stopped again, and I wondered if he were finished. I began to stand up, when he suddenly went on.

"Tragedy and strife often bring people close together. They can create everlasting bonds between those – types of people who never would have gotten together otherwise. That's something I will have the rest of my days with me mates – those alive and those not.

"All I can think is that it was at a heavy cost – those killed and those who remained behind. Sometimes I wonder who was better off …"

Ari's eyes glanced off into the distance, and then he said, "I was at church recently, and my pastor said that goodness is something that transcends the body – that it's part of a man's spirit – a man's soul -- too. That goodness is something that can't be corrupted in this life if it is nurtured within the soul. He said that after we die, that goodness – that purity of the soul -- will continue. I think that may be true, but I also think that part of that everlasting soul is what you leave behind on Earth after you pass on. It you sow goodness while you're alive, others you know and others you love can reap the benefits too. If you are a model for others, then you will have made a mark on society and other people – one that will last for years long after you're dead. Just look at the impact Jesus had on the world, and His impact is still here over two thousand years later.

"So, as I look back on my life, I only hope that it had meaning for those I leave behind. I did what I thought was good – not only for my own soul, but for others whom I loved and cared about. If I am wrong, than I did my best. If I am right, then my family, friends, and perhaps even mankind, will be a little better off than before I was there – walking the earth."

Ari sat down.

"Well done, Ari," I said, with no other words to utter. He had said them all.

I glanced around the coach, and everyone seemed to have a contentment on their faces. They were no longer stressed and impatient but were satisfied with the story and our situation.

At that moment, the doctor came rushing back into the coach. "Come quickly," she said, with urgency in her voice. "Someone is approaching!"

*****

CH 18 Help?

We filed out of the coach as fast as we could, and as we did, we heard the approaching vehicle. We couldn't tell by the lights what it was, but it was coming fast. Instantly, we began waving and shouting for the driver to stop, but soon we put down our hands. The small sports car screamed past us at high speed, swerving to avoid hitting anyone who was standing too far into the road.

Seconds later, we heard a siren – faint at first, but gaining boost rapidly. Flying over the hill were the red and blue lights of another car spinning madly on top. The bobby didn't stop either but continued beyond our position following the first car in hot pursuit. There was no doubt, it was a chase and the officer wasn't about to lose his target regardless of our distress.

"Sh*t!" I heard repeatedly throughout those lining the roadway beside the broken-down coach.

"Now what do we do?" asked the attorney, the first to fall into despair. "We're stuck here forever, and I'll lose my client. This really sucks!"

It was Clara who shouted out, "I hear something – someone else coming. Listen!"

We all became quiet, but I must admit I had a hard time hearing anything.

"Yeah," said one of the young twins, Theresa. "I hear it too."

"What?" I exclaimed, "I don't hear anything!"

However, within a few seconds, even I heard the sounds of another siren in the distance.

"We have to make him stop!" shouted the banker. "Someone has to jump out into the road and wave him down!"

"Yes, quite right," said the attorney, "someone has to get out there and make sure they stop!"

Over the nearby hill, the police car appeared – its red and blue lights too rotating vibrantly in their plastic shells on top of the car. But behind it was another vehicle – one we didn't expect. It was an ambulance.

The bobby pulled off to the side of the road, parking while the ambulance right behind him did the same. Getting out of his patrol car, the officer inserted his baton into the loop on the side of his pants and put on his navy blue cap with a metallic badge on the front even though it was too dark to see what it said.

"Where is the injured party?" the officer asked, coming over to where the bus driver lay. Then, looking down to see the bus driver's condition, he turned and directed the ambulance driver to pull over next to where he was standing. The two EMTs jumped out with their medical bags and rushed over, kneeling and taking out their stethoscopes.

"Was anyone able to get a license plate of the car that hit him?" asked the bobby, looking at the sea of people.

We all shook our heads, somewhat shocked by the question. How did he know the bus driver had been struck? Why wasn't he chasing that other car that had zoomed past only moments earlier? There were too many thoughts going through our heads to answer.

"What about a description?" he asked, hoping for a better answer from us.

Again, we all mumbled, "No."

The officer walked up the road to look at where the incident had happened and scratched his head. Without asking anyone about the incident, he continued to survey the scene, pulling out his notepad and scribbling unseen notes.

While he did this, I approached the doctor.

"How's the bus driver doing?" I asked, genuinely concerned. I hadn't had the time to ask earlier, as I was too intent upon keeping peace inside the coach.

The doctor looked up at me with a quiet, serene countenance.

"It's quite remarkable," she said. "His internal bleeding slowed and then stopped somehow – all on its own. I don't quite understand it, but that's what happened. It was as if someone put their finger on the wound from inside him somehow and stopped the bleeding. Of course, that's quite impossible, but that's my only explanation. He'll be fine, I think. They just need to get him some liquids and take care of his broken bones. He'll live."

"That's great news!" I answered. Then, the officer came over to talk to me.

"We called the bus company. There's another bus on its way from Bristol. It should be here within the next hour. It will take all of you to Waterbury," he said.

"Thanks, I'll let the others know too. They're all worried about getting there."

As the officer turned to walk away, I stopped him. "Officer," I asked, "how did you find out about us? How did you know we were out here?"

"We got a call."

"A call? From whom?"

"Dunno. It was strange. It sounded like a cell phone, but it wasn't. We tried to ping the location but only got the general wooded area around here."

"What did they tell you?" I asked.

"Like I said, it was strange. They said that we'd have a police car in pursuit of a suspected car jacker in the area where your coach broke down. We didn't have any notice or report of a carjacking, but sure enough, within the next ten minutes, Officer Creighton called in a license that matched a carjacking only three hours ago. He took off after the suspect."

"Really?" I pondered. "That is bizarre."

"Yeah, in twenty-two years on the squad, I never had a call like that."

"But how did you know about us?"

"The caller said that we'd find a stranded coach with a bunch of people out here. He said the bus driver had been struck by a hit-and-run, and we'd better bring an ambulance. At first, we didn't believe him, but after Creighton called in, they dispatched me and the ambulance. We came as soon as we could."

"So, it was Manny," I said quietly.

The officer looked at me strangely. "Manny? Who's Manny?" he asked.

"Manny was the man who came out of the woods to help us. He had a backpack and was hiking or camping in the area. He saw we were having problems so he gave us his time and assistance. A really nice guy. Then, he told somebody he was going to get help for us and left. I assume he was the one who contacted you?"

"I don't know," said the officer. "The dispatcher just got a call from a Paul."

"Paul? Who's Paul?" I asked.

"Oh, Paul's a very nice, older gentlemen in town just up the way from here. He must be in his nineties, if not older. He said he had this feeling that something was wrong out here. Some people think he's nuts, but those of us on the force who have known him, know that he's – well, let's just say he's *special*. He sees things, hears things, knows things that we can't explain. It's like he's psychic or something. Anyway, he called in your problem. He seemed to know a lot about it too – the broken-down coach, the accident with the driver – everything. Anyway, you can thank him if there's anyone to thank," said the bobby.

I smiled and looked up to the sky. The night sky was clear and luminous with millions if not billions of stars glowing, twinkling brightly overhead. *Perhaps,* I thought.

*****

CH 19 *Das Ende*

We said our goodbyes. This time, we knew we would certainly never see each other again. But, we were at peace with that. We were at peace with life and what it had dealt us.

Finally arriving at the Waterbury coach station, we all clambered to get off our prison cell. The station itself was small and, at that time of night, was completely abandoned except for the night manager. He didn't even come out from his office inside – instead, letting us fend for ourselves and offering no apologies.

As we grabbed our luggage from the opened compartments below the new coach, I couldn't help but notice almost no interaction between the passengers. It was as though we had never gone through that experience together. Already, their minds had checked out of the past and could only focus on what was next. Tired and looking only to get to my final destination too, there as a big part of me that understood. Yet, I felt there was something more to our plight – something more that we could and should take away from it.

Still, one-by-one those on board scurried off to where they wanted to be. Within only fifteen minutes, nearly all had left the station – either picked up by family or friends or finding other ways to get to a soft pillow and warm comforter for the night.

As for me, I stood as others pulled their black, tan, and gray-zipped luggage from the belly of the bus. At last, I spotted my bags and crouched inside the tombic cell, yanking on my suitcases that were wedged up against a black, equipment bag that must have been intended for coach repairs. Finally, exorcising them, I stood, grips in hand. Standing in front of me was the major. He too was hoping to find his lone duffel in the undercarriage.

"Anything left?" he asked, hopefully.

"Yeah, I think there is one nore piece under there," I answered.

The major ducked inside and pulled out a navy duffel with the insignia of his company on it.

"Got it," he said, smiling.

We began walking away when I said, "Hey, Major?"

"Yeah?"

"Do you feel any differently than when you boarded this coach – well, the other coach – this morning?"

He smiled. "I'm not sure," he answered. "I think so."

"How do you think it changed you?"

"It made me think about …" then he chuckled.

"… the meaning of life?" I inserted.

He laughed again. "Yeah. How did you know?"

"Just a hunch," I said. "Well, take care."

He nodded, threw the duffel over his shoulder and began walking away. I couldn't see where he was going. I didn't see anyone or any car that was waiting for him. It just seemed like he strode through the empty parking lot and disappeared into the night.

I shrugged. It had been a long day, and I was looking forward to getting to my destination too. I was supposed to meet an old friend, and I quickly saw her standing near her car smiling and waving to me. She and I had been colleagues at the university before she had transferred to another college near Waterbury. I still stayed in contact with her, and finally decided to visit her. I guess deep down, she was someone I had always been quite fond of. It was nice that she agreed to have me come and visit.

"Anna," I said, giving her kisses on each cheek, "you're as lovely as ever."

She was, indeed beautiful, and she glowed even though I knew she was tired fro the lateness of the night.

"You'd better say that," she quipped, still smiling. "I would hope for something more than that though, since you've gotten me up in the middle of the night to pick you up at the coach station. Do you know what time it …"

"… yes, and I'm sorry," I said. "I'm really sorry. But there was nothing I could do. We were in the bus, and all of a sudden …"

This time, it was Anna who interrupted, putting her finger to my lips to quiet me. "It's okay. I wouldn't do this for just anyone, you know," she said. "Let's get home. Tomorrow will be another day. I'm so glad you came. I've …"

I looked into her hazel eyes. "You're what?" I asked, when she paused.

She smiled again and looked down. "Let's just get back to my apartment, okay? We can start over tomorrow when both of us are fresh. I've got a few things planned, but mainly I just want to spend some time with you."

"That would be nice," I answered, putting my arm around her.

We walked together toward her car when I got this strange feeling inside of me. I quickly turned around, looking back at the station and the coach. I swear that I saw someone getting out of the bus. He hopped off and glanced in my direction as if he knew I was looking at him. He lifted up the brown cap and waved it at me, grinning as if it had been something he had lost and then found once again. But no sooner than he had lifted his hand in the air with his cap, his image evaporated into thin air.

I blinked once, then twice, making sure I was seeing clearly, but the image of Manny was already gone. As before, he vanished before I could say goodbye.

… *lost and found again*, I thought to myself. Maybe that was what all this was about. The storytelling had been extraordinary, and the experience one that I would forever remember. But what was it that seemed more eternal – more bonding? If I had lost something in my life, then what had I found?

I turned to Anne, and she smiled back, clasping her warm hand around mine. *Perhaps …* I thought *… just perhaps … the meaning of life is just that … Life itself. The good, the bad, the ugly, and then the wonderful. It was all there. But each of us has a different path in life to find it.*

*****

132

Appendix

Word Key

The following table presents which words came from which passenger and which one used them in the story.

CH	Three Words	Story Teller	Words Creator
2	War, wife, mission	Me-History Professor	British soldier
3	Rules, French fries, telephone	Twin sister #1	Government bureaucrat
4	Starving, business, worry	Older Banker	Shopkeeper, husband
5	Bunnies, fantasy, roses	Older actress	Author
6	Friendly, jewelry, cast	Middle-aged policeman	Older actress
6	Peace, Bible, faith	Shopkeeper, wife	Minister
7	Honesty, history, love	Shopkeeper, husband	History Professor
8	Trees, wheels, answers & music, likes, friends	Old woman with Twin sister #2	Engineer
9	Music, likes, friends	Old woman with Twin sister #2	Twin sister #1
9	Balance, Coke, stamps	Business owner	Accountant
10	Image, frame, car	Engineer	Photographer
11	Cool, Jealousy, Lost	Physicist	Twin sister #2
12	Sweat, labor, moon	Minister	Construction Worker
12	Apricots, memories, families	Accountant	Old woman

13	Bobby, crime, rain	Journalist - Photographer	Middle-aged Policeman
13	Atom, math, red	Journalist-Photographer	Physicist
14	Truth, cooking, beggars	Construction worker	Journalist
14	Children, gardening, happiness	Architect	Shopkeeper, wife
15	Colour, essence, Renoir	Gov't Bureaucrat	Painter
16	Structure, anger, creativity	Author	Architect
16	Money, success, tennis	Painter	Business owner
17	Meaning of life	British Soldier	*Unknown*

The Author

Noland Williams has written many novels, typically those with historic relevance or background. He has also contributed several short stories on various topics. Noland T. Williams is a penname used by the author, who lives in Chicago with his family.

Blue M Publishing

Blue M Publishing publishes all books by Mr. Williams and many other authors. You may find other related books on its website at: www.blueMpublishing.com

www.ingramcontent.com/pod-product-compliance
Lightning Source LLC
Chambersburg PA
CBHW060937120626
46557CB00003B/1040